Murder by a Flower

By

TDG

Indian
Head
Rock
Publication

☐

0

Preface

This is a work of fiction. None of the characters are real. Though the states are real, none of the towns are real locations. The events are fictional, as are any circumstances. Any resemblance to a known person, event, or location is purely coincidental. Any similarity to a name, place, company, organization, or event is coincidental, as the entire story is fictional.

The death of a friend and/or family member can be upsetting. Even more so if that death is classified as justifiable homicide. This can attract attention especially if that friend is of a curious sort. Friends and family may learn, what the local law enforcement tried to keep a secret. They begin to question wither, or not it was justifiable. Also, they may question how much a certain law enforcement officer had to do with the murder. If a law enforcement officer was involved, couldn't there be a cover up? In the minds of a family, an unarmed man being shot four times, should have been investigated more rigorously.

Marty was married to Rose, but she wanted to be rid of him. Her problem was that she didn't have any money and they didn't own the house they lived in. It was rented, and they had little to live on. He had a great job, but she wanted to get away from him. She had found another, but he didn't have much either. Marty did have a good life insurance policy, but there was another now that might have some claim to that. She would have to move swiftly to keep the other from having that claim. Rose was unsure as to how she could get rid of her husband and keep all the money that was due to her. Surely putting up with him for nearly four years was worth the money, in his insurance policy. After all, she had three kids to care for, although none of them were his. He didn't even have a place to live till she came along.

A month ago, she wouldn't have thought about this. Not till he got a letter from an old girl, friend of his, saying she had a five-year-old daughter, which was his. The ex-girlfriend also told him she had HIV and that he should be tested. Rose was furious when she read his letter and never abandoned that anger.

The woman two states away that had written the letter, had not heard from Marty and was fearful and angry at him.

She feared she would die and leave her little girl all alone. She did not know how she had contracted HIV. She did think that it possibly, had been her time with Marty. She had known that he was a promiscuous man, but thought at worst she might get VD from him. She had hoped that he would ask her to marry, but that didn't happen, before he had left for Oklahoma. She knew right where he was, as he had talked about home many times with her. In her fear of death, she thought that if he gave her this, he deserved to die too. If he didn't have this disease, he needed to step up and care for his daughter. She had put his name on the birth certificate as father, as she was sure that he was.

Chapter 1

Marty lay in a pool of his own blood. He could barely move, and it was a struggle for him to breathe. He knew that he was dying. He thought *I shouldn't have come here; I knew it could be a trick.* Never in his wildest dreams did he think he might die like this though. Yes, he had thought that he might be killed, but in a bar room brawl; or at least standing facing an opponent on equal footing. He wondered why *am I so cold.* For a time, he thought he might die riding or fighting bulls at a rodeo. Then, while he worked with high voltage for the electric company, he supposed he could die on the job. That nearly happened one night. Now he lay here, dying with four, twenty-two bullets in his gut from his own gun. *Why am I so cold? Is this how death comes?* He could no longer move, and his heart barely beat. His eyes were still open as he heard her say, "It's done, I think he is dead" into the phone. She then called 9-1-1. He heard her exclaim, "My husband, who I have a restraining order against, broke into my house. I had to shoot him. He tried to rape me." Marty's last sight was seeing her in the deputy's arms as they kissed passionately, and he thought, *that's what this was all about."* Then Marty died, laying in his own blood feeling cold and alone.

Years before his dad threatened to kill him. His dad's truck had been wrecked, but it was his brother Billy that had ran it off the road, this time. In all honesty, Marty had taken a turn to fast on icy roads and laid The Truck on its side months before. Kevin had wrecked it once himself, as had their half-brother. This time though, Billy was chasing a girl in a car and lost control, rolling the truck. Between him and his brothers, that old Chevy truck took a beating.

Fortunately, those old Chevy's were tough. This one more than the others though, as they had used sheet metal to make repairs in the past. They would use another truck to pull it upright and drag it home for repairs. Those repairs were always completed by them in their dad's shop. They were great skills they would use for the rest of their lives. Fortunately for them, dad's shop was very well equipped. There were plenty of parts, tools, equipment, and scrap metal to do just about anything. When a neighbor or other farmer needed something repaired, they often worked around the clock fixing equipment for them.

Marty was with his brothers Billy and Kevin driving around their small home town on Saturday night. Billy had talked to this girl, then she got in her car and speeded away. Billy yelled "Let's go boys," as he hopped in behind the wheel.

Yelling "Shotgun," Marty held the door, waiting for Kevin to climb into the center seat. Instead of auguring,

Kevin jumped right in, as he knew they would be left behind if he didn't. Billy laid rubber, as he pressed the gas pedal to the floor. Ahead, the lights of the car faded away as it left town. As the boys left the street lights of the town, they couldn't see her tail lights any more. "She had to turn off," swore Kevin, as Billy braked hard and turned right. Again, Billy floored the gas pedal as they speeded along a gravel road, throwing gravel high in the air behind them. He knew the curve was ahead of them, but he was in it before he expected. All too soon they were in the curve, and Billy turned before he could slow enough to navigate the curve. The rear wheels spun, losing traction on the gravel, and the right side of the truck lifted as they rolled completely over, landing on the wheels in a ditch.

It seemed like hours later they shook off the tumble they had taken. The air was filled with dust and debris as they climbed out of the truck. Their friend Tony Carlton pulled up behind them about the same time. He had seen them peel out of town and followed after them. Tony had gone to school with them and lived a mile and a half down the road. Many times, he was with them on an escapade. Together, they checked out the damage to The Truck. They changed out the front right tire, which had blown. They used a length of pipe, secured from the bed of Tony's truck, to pry the left fender far enough from the tire to make it drivable. Tony followed them to the shop, as he lived only a mile and a half mile away.

They drove The Truck home, parked it in the shop. They had begun working on it when their dad walked in. He looked The Truck over, then turned to face the boys down. Tony had stayed with them helping, till Pop had come in, chewing, them out. Pop threatened to "beat them all to death," before rolling up his sleeves, to help. Once Pop cooled down and rolled up his sleeves, Tony said he had to go home and left. It was nearly dawn before they had the majority of the dents beat out and the torn metal welded together. They would paint it later in the day. They kept

plenty extra cans of paint for it, and had become adept in

spray painting. After a few short hours of sleep and a quick

meal, they were out in the shop finishing repairs on The

Truck. As they worked, they talked about Tony, he was

leaving tomorrow, moving to Texas. He had a job starting

next week as a security guard. He had always wanted to

work in law enforcement, and this was the best way for him

to get started. He couldn't go straight to a trooper or county

agency, without a college education. He couldn't afford the

tuition for college, but there was an opening at this plant,

and they would train him. It was an opportunity for him to

get the training and experience he would need.

The next weekend, Marty and his brothers were going to

the Holdon RCA Rodeo. They planned on going all three

nights and to the rodeo and the dance after. When they

pulled in at the rodeo arena, there was their friend Tim

Gordon. The rascal was sitting on the fence by the bucking

chutes with a cute redhead. As they walked up to them, the two of them turned to look at them, and low and behold, if it wasn't Reba McIntire he was sitting with. She was the singer for the rodeo dance that night and was to sing the National Anthem at the rodeo. Marty was thinking *this will be a great night*. Marty, Billy, and Kevin all three climbed upon the fence on the other side of Reba. They talked about rodeos, country music, and dancing.

After the bronc riding and as the calf roping had just started, their little half-brother Timmy Plumber showed up. He told them that Carl had come home just after they left and was causing trouble. Timmy thought that Carl was probably high and on the run. He had even taken a swing at Mom. The boys weren't about to let that go unopposed.

They decided to go home and take care of Carl together. Tim Gordon asked what was wrong, and Marty told him about Carl and how he was into drugs and always getting into trouble. They were going to run him out of the state.

11

Gordon said, "well let's get her done boys," as they all climbed into The Truck. Once they got home, Pop told them that he had sent Carl packing and, he had left. The last he saw him he was climbing into a cross-country semitruck heading west. They loaded back up and returned to the rodeo. The bull riding hadn't started when they got back to the arena. For all of these guys, the bronc busting, bull dogging, and bull riding was the rodeo. They always enthusiastically watched the other events, but wouldn't willingly miss the bull riding. They definitely didn't want to miss Reba McIntire's performance tonight. Reba was a regular attraction around Oklahoma rodeos and they thought she would make it big one day. She was a great singer and very beautiful.

At the end of the rodeo, they went to the barn across the street for the rodeo dance. They carried with them an ice chest full of ice-cold beer. They were told they would have to leave the ice chest in their truck. By the time they found a place to set down, the music was playing and Reba was singing. Marty popped the top on a beer, took a long swig and turned, looking for a dance partner. He spotted a good-looking burnet and walked up to her. "Ma'am, I believe I promised this dance to you," he said.

"I think not," the lady said as she turned her head to look at Marty. "Perhaps, I'll dance with you anyway" she said, smiling. *He is very cute,* she thought to herself as she got up.

Marty led her out onto the floor, and they began to dance. As they two stepped and twirled around the floor, he whispered in her ear, "I'd like to bite you on the butt, develop, lockjaw, and get dragged to death." She smiled a little at that line. She couldn't believe a guy would come up with something like that. Before the song was over, she agreed to go out to The Truck with him. Hours later, the two of them were still in the seat of the truck, holding tight to each other. They looked up as Billy and Kevin came out,

13

ready to go home. "Well, ma'am I reckon we will be going home now; I'll see you around," Marty said as she climbed out of The Truck. The young lady watched them leave. She hoped to see Marty again, not realizing that he was seventeen and over three years her younger. She thought the other two looked awful handsome too. She would bring a couple of her friends tomorrow night, and *just maybe* she thought to herself.

The boys worked all the next day in the peanut field, chopping weeds. It was a hot day, and they worked through lunch so that they would be able to leave early for the rodeo. That evening they were again at the Holdon Rodeo. Marty went behind the chutes to talk with the bull riders. He had an aspiration to ride bulls himself. He had one more year in school, then he hoped to ride in some of the local open rodeos. Marty and his brothers had already strung a barrel up between two trees to practice on. He was going to earn enough money to buy a bull rope and pay his first entry fee, chopping weeds. Banger Rodeo would be coming up later, and it was an open rodeo. Marty would enter his first bull riding then, he hoped.

Billy was leaving the first of the week, going to Utah. Their father lived there, and he was going to stay with him for a while. Pop was their stepfather. Pop was good to them, but Billy wanted to go see his dad Ryan, and spend time with him. He would work the summer herding cattle up on a mountain range. He would stay at a line shack in Utah near the state line. This was to be the last weekend they would all be together for a while. The plan was to whoop and holler the night away at the dance after the rodeo. The next day was Sunday, and they wouldn't have to work in the field. They would be able to sleep in late. Tonight, though, they would drink, dance, and chase wild women. *That's what we are best at*, thought Marty, *drinking, dancing, and chasing wild women*. Marty had learned that using a vulgar and suggestive line worked for him more often than not. If it didn't work, what the hell, there was always more fish in the sea. Besides, he felt like he was being honest about it that way. He was telling the lady what he wanted straight out.

Pam, Beth, and Shelly were the first ones at the rodeo dance. Pam was telling the others all about Marty and his brothers. They were hoping to dance and have a good time. Pam was eager to see Marty again.

Marty, Billy, and Kevin stopped by The Truck walking from the rodeo to the dance barn. They opened a cooler full of iced down beer and downed one before going on to the dance. Old blue, a blue tick hound, lay in the truck bed to guard the ice chest. That old hound dog wouldn't get out of The Truck or allow anyone but them to get close to it. Though they weren't supposed to carry any beer into the dance, they each had two unopened cans in their jacket pockets. The boys carried empty red solo cups and filled them up once they found a place to sit. As they went through the door, a guard looked at their solo cups. Billy told him, "Spit cups, sir." He made a funny face but waved them on.

Pam spotted the boys as they came in, watching to see where they sat down at. She said "Come on with me," to Beth and Shelly.

"Should we be so bold as to go over there?" asked Beth.

"If we don't, some other girls will snatch them up," stated Pam. They walked to where Marty and his brothers sat. As they approached the table, Marty and his brothers all came to their feet.

"Howdy ma'am," said Marty, "you remember my brothers, Billy and Kevin."

"These are my friends, Beth and Shelly," stated Pam.

"Please have a seat with us ladies," said Kevin as he was eyeing Shelly.

As the band started playing, Marty asked Pam to dance, and they began two-stepping and twirling around the floor. Billy asked Beth to dance as Kevin asked Shelly. The boys were some of the best two-steppers around, and the girls were enjoying the dance with them. Back at the table, Shelly drank a beer offered to her by Kevin. After they had finished the beer, they went out to The Truck to bring in some more, or so they told the others. Kevin and Shelly did return with more beer nearly an hour later. Pam and Beth both refused any beer and were drinking Dr. Pepper. They danced till nearly midnight, when the three girls all left together.

The boys stayed on, and shortly after Pam had exited the door, Marty was up and asking another girl to dance. Other unattached ladies had noticed the three handsome boys and how well they danced. Each of these were anxious for a chance with these boys. All too soon, the band quit playing, and they turned the lights all on to signal closing time.

The boys went out to The Truck. Standing around the back, they each popped a top on another beer. Kevin got the last one, and Billy was left out. Billy grabbed the beer Marty had, saying he didn't need another one. Marty reached with his left hand, as to take the beer back, and then swung with his right hitting Billy on the chin. Billy fell against Kevin, spilling his beer. Kevin turned to Marty and sucker punched him in the gut. After that, it was a free for all amongst the trio. The fight ended as Gordon walked up on them arm in arm with a pretty redhead.

"What's the fight all about this time, boys?" asked Gordon.

Laughing, Billy said, "spilled beer." Then he said, "I guess it's time to go home, boys. Good night, Tim".

"Good night, and ya'll drive safe getting home," said Tim.

The next afternoon, Marty and Kevin drove Billy into

town to catch the bus. He had tickets on Grey Hound from

Banger, Oklahoma, to Vernon, Utah. He would arrive in

Vernon Monday afternoon. He was supposed to spend a

few days at their fathers' house before going up on the

mountain for the summer. Billy was looking forward to

staying in a line shack and taking care of a herd of cattle.

He had talked for months about it, and Marty was wishing

he could go too. They said their goodbyes as Billy climbed

onto the bus.

Chapter 2

Billy was picked up at the Vernon bus station, by his dad,

Ryan. He had only a vague memory of his real father, as it

had been years since he had seen him. They had written

letters a few times, and he had birthday cards each year.

His father was, in spirit and soul, a true old-time cowboy.

He rode herd on cattle and horses, as well as trained the

best working horses around. Some of the horses he trained

won working horse competitions. Ryan also trained some

of the best barrel racing horses, it was a surprise he had

several horses in his stables.

His dad was well known and respected near and far. Ryan was also a mountain man. He had lived his entire life at the foot of these mountains. Many times, he had hunted, fished, and worked in the mountains. More than once, he had spent the winter up on a mountain taking care of livestock. He knew the mountains and respected them; he knew just how dangerous they could be and how fast they could change from beautiful to deadly.

They would be moving cattle up there all week, along with supplies for Billy. Part of the supplies were hay and feed for his horse. They also took plenty of food for him to stay the summer. Billy wasn't to move into the line shack till Sunday afternoon. His dad was going to take him to a rodeo in Colorado a few miles from there Friday night for a last night out, before moving up on the mountain.

On Thursday, Billy and his father hauled the last of the supplies up to the line shack. Billy thought that was a lose description of shack. It was ten feet wide by twenty feet long, with a ten foot by ten-foot enclosure and dirt floor. The remaining half was open to the south with a small pen attached. The enclosure was to keep feed and hay for his horse, with what little room left over for him to sleep in. A small wood stove sat on the south wall. If the weather turned bad, a man could use it to keep warm and cook meals inside the shack. There was a fire ring to the west of the shack where he could cook his meals. A creek ran a few feet away to the south, with a clean spring just up from it to the west. All the comforts of home. Before leaving the mountain, they rode out together and checked on the cattle. They were on the flat Northwest of the shack, grazing contentedly. The job called for Billy to stay with the herd starting Sunday till deer season early in the fall. At that time, the owner of the cattle had to have them all off the mountain according to the contract. Besides, once hunting season started, some of the city hunters might mistake a cow for an elk. The rancher didn't own the range as it was

BLM land, he did have a lease to run livestock for the summer.

Friday afternoon, Billy and his dad went to the rodeo. It was a PRCA rodeo in Colorado, with a dance after. Billy was assured that he wouldn't have a chance to come off the mountain till fall, and he was eager to have a good time that night. It wasn't a long drive, but he had the chance to talk more with his father, Ryan. He had promised that he would come check on him up on the mountain every week or so. He would also bring up anything that Billy might need, including a bottle or two of Crown Royal and chewing tobacco.

The rodeo was a really good one, with great riders and livestock. The dance was in a local nightclub at the edge of town. Ryan paid their way in, and soon they found a small table to sit at. The table was near the restrooms with a good view of the dance floor. They had ordered some beer, and while waiting, Billy spotted the most beautiful girl he had ever seen. She walked right past him on her way to the lady's room. Minutes later, he watched as she walked past him and sat down across the room. Billy was about to get up and ask her to dance when a different girl came up to him, asking if he would like to dance. He went straight out onto the dance floor with her and two-stepped around the floor. At the end of the song, he tipped his hat, saying "Thank you, ma'am." It wasn't by chance that he had guided her around the dance floor, in a manner that left them near the lady he had been watching.

Billy approached the beautiful lady, asking, "ma'am, would you be so kind as to dance with me?"

Cheryl had seen him looking at her as she went to the bathroom. She then watched him dance and thought *this guy is a great dancer.* "I would be pleased to dance with you," she said, as she stood up from her table. Billy led her by the hand out onto the dance floor. They danced and talked, and as the song ended, they were still standing in the middle of the dance floor, looking each other in the eye.

As another song started, Billy said "How about another dance?"

"Sure," she said, "and my name is Cheryl. What is yours?"

"My name is Billy Martin, and it is my pleasure to meet you, ma'am," said Billy.

With a bit of a gasp, Cheryl proclaimed, "my, you sure are polite. Where may I ask are you from? I'm certain you're not from around here."

"No ma'am. Until a few days ago, I lived in Oklahoma, but I live in Utah now," explained Billy.

"What do you do in Utah Billy?" she asked.

"I'm a cowboy for a large rancher."

"Well, that makes sense," she said. They danced and talked till closing time. "Will you be back tomorrow night? I'd really like to see you again."

"Let me ask my dad," he said. "He brought me here, so I don't have any transportation, and I have to be up on the mountain Sunday afternoon."

"I can take you back Sunday morning in time for you to make it up there, if you like," Cheryl offered.

Billy's dad told him if he was back to Vernon by noon Sunday, that would work. Cheryl and Billy left the dance together. At her apartment, he offered to sleep on her sofa. He told her that he only had the clothes on his back though. Cheryl told him to undress, and she would wash his clothes while they slept. As he pulled his shirt off, she was impressed with the rippling muscle tone. Without a thought, she was in his arms, and he was undressing her.

She pulled him to her bedroom, and they collapsed onto the bed.

Billy awoke Saturday morning to the smell of bacon frying. Looking up, he had to think a minute before he remembered where he was. Smiling, he got up and followed his nose to the kitchen. "Good morning, something smells good. Wow, you look even more beautiful in the morning light," Billy said.

"Good morning, and thank you, cowboy."

"If you can take me to a store, I would like to buy an extra pair of jeans and another shirt. I'm going to need them anyway."

Over breakfast, Billy explained what he would be doing up on the mountain for the summer, and that he wouldn't be able to come down till fall. He told her where the line shack was and how primitive it was up there. He told her he would have his horse and would ride out each day to check the cattle. If there were any problems, he had to handle it by himself with what he had in hand.

"You truly are a cowboy, aren't you," Cheryl proclaimed.

"Yes ma'am, I am."

"What family do you have back in Oklahoma?" she asked.

"I have two brothers there and a stepbrother. My mother and stepfather." I have two other brothers around. One, Layne, is working in Texas, the other, Carl, is a drug addict, and I'm not sure where he might be," explained Billy. "My real dad, which you met, lives just outside of Vernon, which is only an hour or so away from here."

"I am pretty sure I've heard of him before. I think a friend of mine bought a horse he trained."

"Could be, he has trained many of the best horses around."

"My friend is a barrel racer and paid a mint for her horse, but it is worth the money."

Billy took Cheryl to a restaurant for lunch, before they returned to her apartment. Later, he wrote a letter to his family and addressed it to his brother Marty. He would share it with the others. He told them he had met a beautiful girl named Cheryl. He also told Marty that he wasn't sure if he would get to see her again. Tomorrow he would be going up on the mountain for the rest of the summer, he wrote. That afternoon, they went to the rodeo together. During the barrel racing, they went to the concession stand for a hamburger.

Once the rodeo was over, they went to the club for the rodeo dance. They sat together and danced most of the night. Cheryl was taken with Billy's dance skills and with his good looks, but even more so by his manners. A lean tall handsome cowboy in a black hat always did catch her eye. Billy was a real cowboy though, unlike some of these

30

drugstore cowboys around, that she had met. While dancing and during the few times they sat down, they talked. They were both interested in the life history of the other. To Cheryl's delight, as she talked, Billy looked deeply into her eyes. She felt that he was truly interested in her and cared about her.

Billy had remembered what his mom had told him, that when a lady talked to him, to look her in the eyes, that was the fastest way to her heart. It seemed to be working for him. Unlike his younger brother Marty, whose tactics went to vulgar pickup lines, Billy depended on his charm. Cheryl really liked this cowboy and was happy she didn't have to use any cheesy lines or movements to attract him, though she seldom had to revert to such tactics.

The next morning, Billy awoke with Cheryl laying in his arms. He slipped out of her bed and quietly dressed. He then mixed up the fixings for omelets. He was cooking the omelets when Cheryl walked up behind him and hugged him from behind. Looking around at her, he was truly amazed at just how beautiful she was. He was certain that Cheryl was the most beautiful woman in the world. "You are so beautiful, I can't believe I am here with you," he said to her.

"You just keep saying that, cowboy."

After breakfast, they showered and got ready to leave. Cheryl drove Billy to Vernon and on to his father's ranch house. He left the letter to Marty with his dad and kissed Cheryl goodbye. "I'm gonna miss you this summer, dear. I'll be dreaming of you every night, of this, I'm certain."

Cheryl walked back to her car, then turned back and said, "I love you, Billy Martin." Then she got in her car and left in a cloud of dust. Billy watched her leave, wondering if he really heard what he thought he heard. For now, though, he had to put those thoughts aside. He had to make certain that he had everything he needed for the months up on the mountain. Looking away from the settling dust of her departing car and up to the mountain, he thought he could even make out the location of the line shack.

By midafternoon, Billy and Ryan were unloading the truck into the shack. He would spend two and a half months alone on this mountain. He had supplies to last him and his horse for the entire summer. His father promised to drive up here and check on him every couple weeks, or so. Billy had a 45 pistol and a henry rifle. With these he could kill some game to eat from time to time or kill any rattlesnakes that might show up. As his dad's truck disappeared over the horizon in a cloud of dust, he had a fire started and a can of beans opened. This, with some tortillas, would be his dinner. He had ridden out while his father finished unloading and checked the cattle. He had already filled a bucket of water for his horse and a canteen for himself.

He had a folding chair to sit next to the fire on, and that was where he was now. Looking around, he could see a mule deer doe with a fawn at the edge of the tree line, up above the creek. They were watching him, unsure if they could come down for a drink. He sat still and watched as they slowly made their way down to the creek. The doe stood watching him twitching her ears as the fawn drank its fill of the cool spring fed water. Then the doe drank as the fawn watched him. Together, they picked at the tender green grass before walking back up the hill to the timber.

The next several weeks were much the same. He would wake up at dawn and feed his horse before he ate breakfast. He had learned early in life that you took care of your horse before yourself. Then he would saddle up and ride out to check the cattle. If any had strayed, he would find them and drive them back to the herd. This is pretty much the way it had been done by cowboys for over a hundred years. The lone cowboy watching over the herd of cattle, caring for their needs. That didn't escape him as he sat tall in the saddle on a rise, overlooking the cattle. He would ride for a short distance, in each direction from the cattle and then back, looking the landscape over. Not far to the south was a deep canyon, he would have to explore it someday. He rode along it, looking for a way down by horseback but never spotted one. That meant he might have to hike down there sometime.

One day he did make the hike, to find a river flowing through the canyon and plenty of game. He saw bear tracks and mountain lion tracks. He also found several torn deer carcasses, that looked to be lion kills. He was glad he had brought along both the forty-five and the henry. He climbed back out of the canyon at a rock slide, which came out not far from the line shack.

Five weeks after she had dropped Billy off, Cheryl decided to go see if she could find him up on that mountain. She left very early one morning, going to Ryan's ranch house, hoping he was home. She thought she could find the mountain line shack but wasn't sure. Nor was she sure if her car could make it on the off-road trails up on the mountain. She did know that Ryan could help her. Cheryl wasn't surprised to see Ryan out in the corral with a horse when she arrived just after dawn. After she explained what she wanted, Ryan smiled and suggested they load this horse and go up and see Billy. He needed to ride this horse for a couple hours, and what better place than up on the mountain. He loaded an ice chest of beer in the back of his truck and loaded the horse in the trailer. He also grabbed a bag full of supplies he had been gathering for Billy.

Billy had returned to the line shack and rubbed down his horse before putting him in the stable. He was gathering some firewood when he heard the truck coming. He looked up to see his dad's truck with a trailer behind it. A little later, the truck pulled up, and Cheryl jumped out and ran to him, grinning from ear to ear. She was wearing boots and tight blue jeans that complimented her long legs wonderfully. She wore a low-cut western blouse with a leather jacket over. Her long black hair was tied in a ponytail, right below her black hat. Her beauty nearly took his breath away. He had thought of her every night since the weekend he had spent with her. Here, this beautiful mountain girl was with him on top of the mountain. *It was a dream come true,* he thought to himself. *How can I get so lucky.* "Hello, beautiful," he said.

"I told you to just keep saying that, didn't I?" she asked.

Billy built up a fire and offered her the chair to sit in. Ryan unloaded the horse, saddled it up, and excused himself after unloading the ice chest full of beer and the bag of supplies. Ryan was going to ride some of the roughness off the young colt as part of his training. Ryan liked riding up here in the fresh air and grandeur scenery. Not long after Ryan had left, Billy led Cheryl into the shack. An hour later, they came out of the shack and sat together on a blanket near the fire. They were like this when Ryan came back. After loading the horse, Ryan told

Cheryl he had to go back home, and unless she wanted to stay up here for a couple weeks, she had to leave with him. "Oh, I would love to stay up here, but I have a job to get back to," she said.

Ryan visited every couple weeks at least, and sometimes more often. Many times, he would bring a horse he was training, and they would ride together. Cheryl came up two more times during the summer and those times were the highlight of Billy's summer up there on the mountain. One time that Cheryl was there, they left Ryan at the camp as they rode the horses. Billy was amazed at her ability to ride. She was a natural on horseback and riding in the mountains. She went down one slope that he wouldn't try. He watched as she laid back on her mount and kicked spurs, sending her mount down a steep slope. He went around to an easier trail down into the draw to meet her. "You're an amazing rider," he told her.

"I'm a mountain girl and practically raised on the back of a horse," she told him.

The owner of the cattle came out in the early fall to check with him. He told Billy that he was preparing to move the cattle down off the mountain for the winter. Two days later, Ryan pulled up with his trailer behind the truck and another truck following. The owner came with Ryan, and he would help Billy move off the mountain. The owner was happy with the cattle and Billy's work, so he wrote him a check for the summer's work. Billy thanked him and watched him ride away in his fancy truck. They loaded up Billy's horse and things before heading back down the mountain. As they went past the cattle pens, where Billy had rounded up all the cattle, they saw the owner and his men loading the cattle up on semi-trucks. In a couple hours, they would have the cattle all off the mountain.

After a few days helping his dad, Billy borrowed his dad's old car to go to Colorado. He was going to go see

Cheryl. A week after that, Billy and Cheryl showed back up at Ryan's, and they were married. They had brought Ryan's car back, and she had followed in her car. Their plan was to go back to her place, load up all her belongings, and move back to Oklahoma.

Billy had heard from Kevin, and he had an oilfield job for Billy, if he could get back there in three days. He would go to work with Kevin for Carter, a guy they both knew, who was a pusher on a drilling rig. Kevin knew about a trailer house that was for rent. They could live there, and it was only a few miles from the rest of the family. Not that they had much, but everything they owned was in the car and a small U-Haul trailer behind it. They took turns driving and only stopped for fuel and to eat. Cheryl had been apprehensive and yet excited to marry and move away with Billy. He was a true cowboy and exciting to be with. It didn't hurt a bit that he was so handsome. She had never been around a young man that was so polite and respectful.

This really impressed her. Now she was leaving home and everyone that she knew, to be with him. It was exciting while, being intimidating too. *This was marriage* she thought. She hoped that it would be as great as she had dreamed it would be.

Chapter 3

Marty had come in from the field with the rest of the family at sunset. They had worked all day hoeing weeds out of the peanuts. He walked out to the mailbox while his mom started supper and Kevin started the chores. Marty sat down, tearing open the envelope addressed to him. Pop asked why he wasn't helping Kevin. Then he noticed that Marty had a letter he was reading. "Hey, Pop, it's a letter from Billy. Billy wrote that he was all ready to go up on the mountain for the summer and that he had met a girl named

Cheryl. He promised to write or call in the fall when he came off the mountain. Till then, though, he would be out of communication."

   The summer went fast for Marty, as he worked most of the time in the field. He had earned enough money to buy a bull rope and all the gear he needed to ride in the Rodeo. He had sent in his entry fee and signed up for the Banger rodeo a couple weeks before school started back. Kevin was running around with some older boys that worked in the oilfield. He was there to chop weeds, but any free time he was off running around. Marty worked out on the barrel and doing pushups along with chin-ups. Marty was the shortest of his brothers, but he was beginning to build up his upper body strength. He had been working all summer exercising in the methods the bull riders he had talked to, suggested. Now he thought himself ready. Marty didn't play summer baseball as he had to work in the field. Summer ball they played nearly every day. He needed to work to help the family and to earn the money he needed. What money he earned he saved for entry fees and for spending money. He knew he would need that money, once he started going to the rodeos.

He was signed up for Friday night at the Banger Rodeo. It was a week before school was to start. Kevin went with him, and as they pulled up to the area, there was Tim Gordon. He was

directing traffic into and around the area from the middle of the highway. Marty yelled out, "Hey Tim I'm riding tonight," as they pulled in.

Later, Marty had placed his gear behind the bucking chutes and was stretching by the gate. Tim came by and said, "Did I hear you say you were riding tonight?"

"Yeah. I'm riding bulls tonight. I drew one called Black Demon," said Marty.

"Well good luck. Do you have anyone to help you?"

"Yep, Kevin is with me, and he'll help me pull in. What were you doing out in the middle of the road anyway?"

"Jerry, who runs this rodeo, is a friend of mine and asked me to help out. I've helped out directing traffic at the annual meeting the last couple years, so that's what I was doing."

"Are you sticking around for the dance after?"

"Of course, I'm sure you are too, aren't you?"

Marty laughed and said, "Certainly and after riding a bull, I'm sure to get a dance from every girl here. They won't be able to resist me."

"Well, Marty, you better get ready for your ride, and I'll see you later. Looks like they're pushing your bull to the front of the line. I'll be watching you from the stands," said Tim as he walked away.

Marty climbed aboard his ride and pulled the rope around

the bull. Kevin used a metal rod with a hook on it to pull

the rope under the bull's belly. The rope was pulled tight

and looped over Marty's right gloved hand. His glove and

the rope had been rosined. Marty heard the announcer say

that the first rider up was a local boy on his first bull. Marty

nodded at the gate attendant and laid back with his left

hand high in the air. As the gate opened, the bull reared up

and twisted out of the chute, Marty's feet were high up over

the bull's shoulder, and he raked down with his spurs as the

bull came down on his front hooves. Marty had scored the

bull out so far; it was a clean ride. Marty didn't think of this

yet, as he was watching the bull's shoulders for an

indication of his next move. Marty saw the bull's left

shoulder rise and the right dip, so he leaned to the right,

expecting a right turn. Sure enough, the bull went that way.

Marty stayed with the bull for just over seven seconds, then

he lost his balance as the bull came out of a spin before

expected. Marty hit the ground hard, but got up fast, running for the fence. He was sure he heard the buzzer after he hit the ground. From on top of the fence, he looked at the scoreboard, to see no points. There went his hundred-dollar entry fee. His only consolation was the applause and any girls that might be motivated by his ride. He looked around at the crowd after that and saw a beautiful blonde watching him, smiling. He smiled back and tipped his hat at her. Then he jumped off the fence and went behind the chutes.

Marty gathered his gear into his bag and placed it in The Truck. He and Kevin carried their ice chest into the barn by the rodeo area. The rodeo dance would be in the barn, and no one was paying any attention to a bull rider with an ice chest tonight. There was no table or chairs, but there were plenty of hay bales, set up in rows to sit on. They placed their ice chest behind a bale of hay and sat down. Marty popped the top on a can of beer and looked around. He spotted several likely girls, and they were looking back at him.

Tim Gordon walked up, sitting a small ice chest behind the hay and sat down. "That was a good ride, it's a shame you didn't make the buzzer," Tim stated. "Next time, maybe you'll get in the money."

"I hope, it'll get expensive if I don't."

As the music started, Marty got up and walked to a young lady and asked her to dance. Tim spotted a girl he knew and asked her to dance. By the time the band played their last song, Marty had danced with every single girl and many of the married ones too. His beer was all gone, and he was ready to go home, it had been a long day. He had asked the stock contractor where their next rodeo was and if they had any open slots for bull riding. He learned that they were going to Thames next weekend, and they had a couple openings for Saturday night. Marty paid up the fee and told

48

Kevin and Tim that he was riding there and when. Tim said he would come watch him unless he had to work. He was working for the electric company and was on call all the time.

The weekend of the Thames rodeo Marty was there, ready to ride on Saturday night. He had been disappointed to learn that there wasn't a rodeo dance after. Tim was there to watch him ride and talked with him for a while before the rodeo started. Kevin helped him rig up on his bull, and this time he covered his bull. He scored in the money this time barely, but enough to pay for this entry, his last entry and a good start on his next fee. Tim congratulated him on his ride and asked what they were doing after the rodeo. Since they weren't sure, he told them about a place they could go to and how to get there.

This was a BYOB club, and any age could enter. There was a door charge, but it wasn't too high. Even though there was an age limit on bringing in beer, no one was checking ice chests. After sitting down Marty even noticed several people with open bottles of whiskey passing them around. There was a good band playing, and a lot of pretty girls looking to dance. Marty and Kevin planned on having a really good night. Monday school started back, and they wouldn't have much chance for fun till spring. Once school started, they would be tied down with school work and after school chores. There were also fairs coming up, along with stock shows and ball games. Marty was on the fall baseball team and had a really good batting average. He could run the bases good as well.

By the third week of school, Kevin was in trouble and had to stay home for a week. Kevin told Mom and Pop that he wasn't going back to school, he was going to work for his friend Carter. He didn't care if Kevin had a diploma or not, just a strong back and willingness to work hard. Kevin was eager for the job and the pay that came with it. The rig wasn't far away, and he could go home between shifts.

Marty was still in school and doing okay there. He had

several good friends and played on the baseball team. Word

had gotten around the school that he was riding bulls in the

rodeos, and that added to his status among his peers.

Baseball season would soon be over, and basketball would

start soon after. They were already practicing, and Marty

would make first string.

Kevin was working a week on and a week off now. He

was home alone on his off time, when the phone rang. He

answered the phone to hear his brother Billy on the other

end. Billy told him he had gotten married, and they were

thinking about coming back to Oklahoma. Kevin told him

he could probably get a job for him on the drilling rig.

Carter was looking for another good hand. They had just

promoted one of his hands up to tool pusher and gave him

his own crew. Both crews were needing more hands. Kevin

also told Billy that he knew of an old trailer house that was

for rent near home. It wasn't fancy, but it had a little

acreage with it. The trailer was off the highway far enough

to give them some privacy.

That night, after everyone was home, Kevin told them all

that Billy was coming back to Oklahoma and he had a new

wife. They were all excited to see Billy again and meet his

bride. Pop said he would go check on the trailer for rent

and see if it was a good deal for the newlyweds. It would be

a couple days before Billy and Cheryl left Colorado, and

would take all the next day driving for them to get there.

Mom, Pop and the boys would work on the trailer if

needed, to fix it up for Billy and Cheryl. Kevin had already

called Carter and told him about his older brother, and

Carter agreed to hire him. Carter had said "If he works

anything like you, he'll be a good hand." That settles it,

Billy would have a good job as soon as he got there, if he

wanted it.

They patched up a hole in the floor and covered it with

some used carpet. They got the power turned on, and with

that, the water well. This allowed them to check out the plumbing. It all seemed to work. The back door needed some repairs, and they took care of that. Marty's mother cleaned for two days trying to make it look good for the new bride. There was a cook stove and a refrigerator, and they both worked. The refrigerator needed a lot of cleaning, though their mother cleaned it thoroughly with Clorox bleach.

Marty had just arrived home from school and finished his chores when a strange car pulled in. He noticed that it had Colorado plates and knew it must be Billy and his wife. Marty yelled at the house "Hey Billy's here." He then met Billy in front of the car as they parked. Marty shook Billy's hand before turning to look Cheryl over. With a whistle, he said, "Wow, she's a looker. How did you rate her, Billy?" Then Marty hugged Cheryl tightly and kissed her on the lips. She blushed, but not much, as Billy had warned her about his brothers. They walked to the back porch and were met by Mom, Pop, and Kevin. Mom had been expecting them and already had a big meal cooking. Kevin gave Cheryl a big hug and kissed her too, as Marty said, "I beat you to it, Kevin."

They talked for a while before Pop took them to the trailer house. It wasn't as nice as Cheryl 's apartment had been, but it was bigger. She could tell that they had been working on it for her. They did have ten acres to go with it, which would be big enough for a couple horses. Ryan had promised them a trained working horse once they got settled in. Cheryl was eager to have her own horse again, as she was an experienced rider. After looking the house over, the newlyweds were satisfied with it. Before long they would make it their home. That night they went back to Mom and Pops house for dinner and talked about the summer and their wedding. Later, they returned to their new home. Their first night alone in their new home. Billy even picked her up on the porch and carried her inside.

Might sound corny, she thought, *but it was romantic.*

The next day, Marty went back to school, and his friends there had many questions for him. They knew Billy and wanted to know about his new wife. It was his senior year, and he was determined to graduate. Kevin should have graduated the year before but had dropped a grade. That was part of the reason he was eager to quit school. A few days later Kevin, and Billy went to work with Carter on the drilling rig. This left Cheryl alone at home, cleaning and working on the trailer. After a few days, she was getting the trailer house the way she wanted it. Each time Billy came home, he noticed the work she had completed and even as tired as he was, he complimented her for it.

On Billy's days off, they worked together on the fences around their property. Then they built a small shed for horses, hay, and feed storage. It took them a while, but they enjoyed the time working together. Soon they had everything fixed like they wanted. Billy had told her he didn't need much, as he had her.

At spring break, Billy was off work and had talked to Ryan about the horse. Billy had enough money now that he wanted to buy a second horse from his dad for Cheryl. They planned on pulling a trailer up there and bringing both horses home with them. Marty asked if he could go along, as he had the week off from school. They thought it was a good idea and agreed to take him along. They could go straight through, taking turns driving. They spent the night with Ryan and returned with the two horses the next day. They had picked out places to stop on the way home, so they could unload the horses and walk them around. Billy and Cheryl now had horses they could ride. Marty had a chance to visit his dad and make plans for the coming summer. After talking to Billy about the summer he spent on the mountain and then talking to his dad, Marty was anxious to go. For Marty, it sounded like a great adventure

and opportunity.

Chapter 4

The year rolled on, and soon it was almost time for Marty to graduate. Mom was wanting a job of her own, as the boys were growing up and moving out. Pop and Mom bought the corner store and service station just down the road. It was in the country at an intersection of two highways. When there weren't other chores to do, Marty worked in the store with her. Cheryl too, started working in the store, as well as Billy and Kevin when they weren't away on the oil rig. The rig had moved across the state, so they now worked away for two weeks and came home for two weeks.

Some days Marty got off the school bus at the store, but his mom made him do his homework behind the counter. Before closing, she would make him sweep the floors and help stock the shelves. They often ate dinner at the store, and even Pop would come by to eat. There was a grill behind the counter they could cook hamburgers on and a deep fat fryer. They had two booth tables near the entrance and often had people stop for a meal. Marty learned really quick how to cook up a meal on the grill and fryer.

Not long after that, Tim Gordon rented the house right across the road from the store. It was a one-bedroom, flat topped, cinder block house. It had been a restaurant back in the day, but was converted into a rental house. They called the house the hole in the wall, as twice cars had lost control at the intersection and ran into the house.

While working at the store, Cheryl had a man talk to her about a job in Oklahoma City. He worked for a model agency and was looking for new faces. They set an appointment for her to audition, and she asked Mom to go with her. Once they got to the location, it was obvious that it was a legitimate business. She easily got the job and was soon working as a model for the agency. Most of the time, she modeled for local business advertisements. One of her best paid advertisements was for a car dealership. She stood by the cars wearing hot pants, high heels, and a halter top. She was uncomfortable in the heels, but she had to admit the photo looked good, though it was hard to recognize her with all the makeup. She was used to wearing makeup, but not as much as they put on her for the photographs.

One weekend, Marty and Kenny came up with a bright idea. They would go to Texas and get some stronger beer. Mom had left them to close the store, and they locked up on time. Kenny emptied out the cash register, placing the cash in his pocket. They drove to the Texas line and crossed over to find an open store. They spent all the cash for out of state beer.

Next morning Mom opened the store to find them leaning against the walk-in refrigerator door, passed out with empty cans laying everywhere. When she asked about the cash from the drawer, they told her it was in the walk-in. All in illegal beer. They sold all the beer out the back door to guys they knew, in two days and paid their mom back.

Marty graduated from high school and made arrangements to go to his father's place in Utah for the summer. Ryan had offered to help him get a job watching cattle on the mountain like Billy had done, which sounded great to Marty. In his mind, he thought that he would be able to get in some bull riding experience while he was up there. Marty caught the bus in Banger and left for Utah. All the way up there he thought about the stories Billy had told him and his chance to cowboy all summer.

Marty arrived at the bus station in Utah and was met by his dad, Ryan. He settled in with his dad and even bucked out some green horses for him. Ryan took Marty to the local rodeo, where Marty had entered, and he won. Just over a week later, the day came for Marty to move up on the mountain. He would spend the summer up there alone, or at least he thought at the time. Marty had never been up to the mountains, and to him, they looked magnificent. The air was clean and fresh. The flats had sage brush and often enough, you could see mule deer laying hidden in the sage. The mountains to the north rose steadily and still had snow covered peaks. His dad had told him that the other side dropped suddenly into the Flaming Gorge across the Wyoming border. He also told Marty that only for a month or so in midsummer, did the snow melt completely off their peaks. From the top of the hill, it was three miles to the nearest manmade object, other than the shack. That was the highway going north to Wyoming. The gate coming off the highway opened onto the trail to the line shack. Just off the highway were the cattle pens and loading chutes for loading and unloading the cattle.

Marty had a good horse and saddle, plenty of food for himself to last till fall, and feed for the horse. He also had his Winchester rifle and a colt pistol. His horse was green, broke, and needed daily riding before it would be trained enough to sell. That was part of his task for his dad, to ride the horse each day. The summer went well, and he rode out, checking cattle daily. His dad came to visit every couple weeks or so, for a while. Then he didn't show up for a month. Marty was worried about it, but there was nothing he could do about it. Though Marty didn't mind being alone, week after week went by without seeing another human, or having anyone to talk to. Finally, his dad's truck came into view, coming along the ridge road. Marty was riding along the opposant ridge when he spotted the truck. He rode down to the shack to meet his father.

Marty rode up to see a woman he didn't know helping his dad out of the passenger side of the truck. He had been thrown by a young bronc and broken his leg. He was healing, but slowly. Ryan told Marty that he would be back in time to move Marty off the mountain. As soon as he heard from the cattlemen, whose livestock Marty was watching, he would come back, even if his friend had to drive him up here again. They stayed and talked for two hours, and Marty unloaded some extra supplies Ryan had brought with him along with a letter from Oklahoma. Marty wrote a reply to the letter to send back with Ryan to mail for him. As Ryan left, he promised to be back by fall, but that never happened.

Just over a week later, Marty watched as herds of elk moved off the high mountains from the North going south past him. The mule deer were out feeding around the clock, as were the cattle. An hour before sunset, the wind changed to the North, and the temperature dropped below freezing.

He built up his fire and fed his horse before curling up for the night. Marty woke up the next morning to find three feet of snow on the ground. He thought, *the cattle and I were supposed to be out of here, before this happened. I wonder how long before they are able to come get me.*

Marty fed his horse, then dug out some firewood to start a fire. He had to shovel snow away from the fire pit and get dry kindling from inside the shed before he could get a fire going. Next problem was getting water. He had enough for this morning in the shed, but he would have to carry more up from the spring. Even that presented a problem, as the spring was covered in snow. After digging through the snow at the spring, he found running water underneath. He would have to keep it inside the shed along with some firewood to keep dry. By this time, he had to add more wood to the fire. It was already obvious to him; he would have to spend much of his time cutting and hauling firewood. Midday, he saddled up and rode out looking for the cattle. He found them downstream of the creek, just around the bend from the shack. They were partially sheltered from the elements here and were able to access water in the creek. Though there was little for them to eat, he had hay, and a little feed left for his horse, but not enough for the cattle.

The next day, the snow was just as deep. Marty got a fire going and stroked it up to a blaze. He saddled his horse and checked on the cattle. He found them near the same location and then rode up the hill to a stand of Quakes. There were plenty of fallen trees he had noticed before the snow. After kicking the snow back, he found a fallen tree and tied his lariat to it. He then threw a dally around his saddle horn and dragged the log back to the shack. He rubbed down, then fed and watered his horse before he started cutting and chopping the wood. He would make three more such trips this day and most days after. The next night, he got up twice during the night to add wood to the fire. The last time it was snowing again.

The next morning, he awoke to find the snow nearly up to his shoulders. He was now sure it would be a long time before anyone could get to him or the cattle. He had checked his supplies and was certain that he would run out of food in three weeks, and the same with the feed for his horse. Unless feed or grazing was found the cattle, they wouldn't last but a few more days.

Marty remembered watching a movie where the main character found himself in the mountains after the snow fell. It was mid spring before it thawed out in that movie. One of the first things he did was to make some snow shoes. On his next trip to get firewood, he cut a couple small saplings and brought them along with the logs and some green twigs. After he built up a big blazing fire, he bowed the saplings into two large teardrop shaped snowshoes. He peeled narrow strips of bark, then braided them together into twine. He used the twine and smaller twigs to lace the snowshoes. The cattle were still in the same place all hunkered down together, they were beginning to get in a bad way. He had a good enough trail to their location and to the tree stand to ride through. Going anywhere else by horseback was out of the question. He had an idea about walking to the large canyon to see what it looked like. Maybe there would be open grass down there just, maybe. If there was, he would have to find a way to drive the cattle down there.

Early in the morning, Marty built up a big fire then fed his horse. He had cut back on the feed, trying to stretch his supplies. He started out walking with his snowshoes to the canyon. It took him twice as long to get there than it would have if not for the snow. What he found was very discouraging. As far as he could see, everything was covered in deep snow. Sadly, he turned back to the shack. In a patch of evergreens not far from his shack, he spotted a young mule deer buck. He had his pistol with him. *I wish I had my rifle, but just maybe I can slip in close enough for this pistol,* he thought. The wind was in his favor, so he moved as quietly as he could, getting closer to the buck. Very gently, he pulled the pistol out and aimed it, and boom, he had a buck. Fortunately, it was downhill from here to the shack, as the buck was heavy. After a while, he got it to his camp and hung it in a tree. He didn't need a freezer here, but he did need to get all the meat taken care of and placed so that it didn't draw attention to other animals. There were bears around here and mountain lions. The bears should be hibernating, but the lions would be hungry, and the smell of game would attract them, if he didn't get the meat cared for right. That evening, he enjoyed a big deer steak. While eating his steak, he thought about the cattle. He had something to eat, but they didn't.

Another morning, and still the snow was just as deep, if not deeper. Marty got up and began his morning routine.

He saddled the horse to check the cattle and drag in some

more logs for firewood. He was just riding out of the camp

when he heard a low flying airplane. He looked around and

spotted a twin-engine airplane flying low towards him. The

plane circled around him, so he figured it might be the

cattle owners. He waved and then pointed towards where

the cattle were. As he rounded the bend, he saw the plane

drop down low and someone kick out some hay for the

cattle. They made four passes kicking out hay. The plane

rose out of the valley, climbing before turning down off the

mountain. The cattle had feed for a few days now, but soon

all he would have would be that deer meat. The cattle had

been stomping at a hole in the creek, keeping it open

enough for them to get water to drink.

Marty picked up a square of hay for his horse as he was

dragging logs back to camp. He would put the portion away

for his horse. Again, he spent most of the day cutting

firewood. He had placed the deer meat in empty airtight

containers that his rations had been in. He was filling the water containers every afternoon late, so to be sure to have water, if the spring froze over. He had never spent a winter up in the mountains before, so he was worried. He had heard stories about what to do and watched old westerns with mountain men. If he could stay warm and keep something to eat and drink, he could survive. *Boy, will I have a story to tell,* he thought. Then he thought *this is going to be tough though, and I don't know if the cattle can make it.*

Almost weekly, the plane came to drop hay for the cattle. Marty continued to watch them and pointed to the herd when the plane came. On the second week, he was out of supplies, all he had to eat was a little of the deer meat. The only thing he had for his horse was some of the hay he had picked up from the drops. On the third drop, the plane dipped down low over the shack and dropped a package and a bundle with a homemade parachute. The package had dried food for him along with a letter from his father and warm clothing. Wrapped in the clothing were two bottles of Crown Royal. The bundle had two bags of oats for his horse. He was ecstatic with joy over the supplies. He watched as the plane dipped over the cattle to drop more hay for them.

In the letter from Ryan, he learned that the early winter snow had caught everyone by surprise including the cattlemen. Ryan also told him they would get him out, if possible, but that when a big snow like this comes, it usually was impossible to get up there. Ryan would continue to send supplies to him as long as the cattlemen sent a plane of hay for the cattle. At some point, they might write off the herd and stop. The plane cost a bundle of money. Marty learned that it could be the middle of March, if not later, before the thaw. Tomorrow was the first day of October. He might have to spend half a year up here in a frozen wasteland. Marty opened the first bottle of Crown and took a long hard swig. He then put it away, as these two bottles might have to last him all winter.

Morning came all too early, each night when Marty curled up in his blankets and got warm, he would think, *I should be like the bears and just hibernate till spring.* Morning came, and he would crawl out of the blankets, build up the fire, and fix breakfast. The chores became a routine now, along with bringing in firewood. He was building head high piles of wood now along the north and west sides of the shack and fire pit area. One saving grace for him was a small wood stove with a chimney inside the shack. If not for that, the water he brought up in the afternoons would freeze. One day he had a break from the dried food, beans, rice, tortillas, and such, along with the deer meat. He was able to kill a couple quail in the timber. He had found them while he was getting logs for firewood. That evening, before dark, he cooked them slowly over the open fire pit. He had dug out some sage brush from the snow and crumbled it in his hands, then rubbed the quail with it, before cooking them over an open fire. They were like a feast for him.

The days and then the weeks passed, Marty wasn't sure of what day it was anymore. He was now sure though, that it had been nearly two weeks since the plane had come. He wondered if they had given up on the herd of cattle. The cattle had moved out of the creek bottom after the third week, going into the evergreens. Another week after some had started staying away from the big herd, into a half dozen smaller herds. In the deep snow, it was impossible for him to keep track of them all now. He still wasn't able to ride his horse except along broken trails. The snow was just too deep. The last two times the plane came, his dad had sent larger amounts of supplies for him and his horse. If the plane didn't come back, he might have enough now to last, if spring came early.

Twice when he was out looking for the cattle and getting wood, he saw a mountain lion stalking him. Once he fired a shot near it to scare it off. *Maybe I should have shot the lion instead of scaring it. I remember hearing or reading that mountain lion is the best meat to eat* he thought to himself. He decided if the cat came around again looking to him for a meal, he would make a meal out of it. Eat, feed his horse, look for cattle, cut firewood, carry water, and all that time watching for game, this was Marty's survival task and daily routine. Cold, it seemed like he was always cold now. He couldn't remember being warm any more. Standing or sitting around a blazing fire, one side might warm up, but the other side would be freezing. As fast as he turned to warm the other side, the one would be cold again.

As the days got even shorter, they got colder. He now had plenty of firewood but brought back more when he did go out. He was sure now, no one was coming for him or the livestock till spring. Marty wasn't sure if he would survive.

75

He had piled some of the firewood in front of the horse shed, providing his horse with a little more shelter. He had left a narrow opening, which the horse could go in and out of. There were days now that he saw some cattle and days that he didn't, so he knew some were still alive. He had seen some eating small sapling trees sticking up through the snow and chewing bark off of trees.

It seemed like the days were starting to get longer, but, if at all possible, it seemed colder. He thought that it had to be after Christmas now and going into the coldest part of winter. Marty still had food for himself and feed for his horse, but wasn't sure if it would last. He hadn't seen a deer or any game in a long time now. He was watching a calf that seemed to be all alone, for two days, it had been near the camp with no other cattle around. He had gone out trying to track it or find a cow it belonged to. Finally, he found her lying dead in the snow, half buried by the cold fluff. He knew then, the calf wouldn't make it. When he got back, he shot it in the head and butchered it for the meat. Beef loin steak for dinner that night left him desiring a baked potato to go with it. Even as cold as it was, he could go for an ice-cold beer. He settled for a long draw off the second bottle of Crown. Looking at the half empty bottle, he thought, *I'll have to go easy on this, or it won't last till spring.*

The snow now was to the top of his shed, a good thing about that was it helped keep it warm. He had trails that he had kept shoveled out from the shack to the fire pit and to the spring. Between the shoveling and the big blazing fire he kept going, he had a nice area around the fire ring more or less clear. He had tried making an igloo with the snow he shoveled away from his trails. After the best attempt, he tried building a fire inside, thinking he might make a smoke house. He did something wrong as the fire melted the snow, which then drowned the fire.

Finally, it warmed up one day. *Oh, the sun felt so good.* Some snow melted, but it was still very deep. Marty had learned to watch closely where he walked. There were places you could step off that might look level, but you could drop over your head in deep snow. It froze that night, and every bit of water from the melted snow turned to ice. The next day, it warmed up again, and more snow melted. He thought he was going to make it. If the snow continued to melt, he would be able to ride out soon to look for any cattle that might have survived.

Six days later, the snow was down enough, he could look for cattle and check out the road into the line shack. Eagerly, he saddled his horse. The horse wasn't nearly as eager, though, and bucked with him for a bit. They got it together and rode out looking for cattle. The road was still impassible, too much snow and very muddy underneath. It would be several days of sunshine before anyone could get even a four wheeled drive in here. He rode on, looking for any signs of cattle. He found a small herd in the timber near the canyon. He left them there and rode on. Later, he found a larger herd on the flat, eating at the sage brush. Marty decided to keep looking tomorrow and try to drive the smaller herd to the larger one.

Marty found two more small herds, and the next day, pushed them all together. He then started pushing them closer to the pens. There was more grass for them to graze on near the pens. A few days later, it dried up enough for trucks to come and go. The owners came to count the cattle, there was only about one quarter of the herd left. Ryan came with his truck and trailer to haul Marty and his horse home. Ryan had to stop on top of the hill as the narrow trail down to the shack was still too slick to drive down and back up. Marty rode his horse up the steep hill and loaded him into the trailer. On the way down the mountain to Vernon, Ryan told Marty that the cattle owners weren't going to pay him. They had lost too many cattle and spent too much money to fly the hay up there. Ryan told him that the last two flights he had paid for the fuel, so he could send the supplies for Marty, to help him survive through the winter. Ryan had used all his savings to pay for that fuel. Ryan told Marty that he could rest up for a week or so, whoop it up, then go back up the mountain for the summer to earn the money for a start. Marty said, "No way, I'm getting out of here as soon as I'm able."

"How are you going to do that, son? You're broke and don't even have money for a bus fare."

"I don't know how I'll do it, but if I have to, I will hitch a ride to Oklahoma," stated Marty.

That night, Marty went to the bar and hung one over. The next day was Wednesday, and he called an old friend that evening. "Hello Tim, this is Marty. Can you help me get out of Utah? I had to spend all winter in the line shack up on the mountain and want out of here now. Okay, I don't know how, but I'll pay you back."

Tim bought an airline ticket for his friend Marty and had them hold it at Salt Lake City Airport. The airline ticket for Marty was waiting for him at Salt Lake City airport for 6:00 Friday morning. Friday night, he would be back where it was warm. He found a ride to Salt Lake Thursday and left Vernon with a small carry bag and his saddle. His ride dropped him off at the airport, and he spent the night in the lobby, sleeping on the floor, his head on the saddle. At least it was warm here, and he was on his way back to Oklahoma. He could hardly wait and was so excited, he could hardly sleep. Finally, he fell asleep, but awakened to the speakers announcing flights the next morning. He heard his flight number called and got up and ready before going to the right gate. This was his first time on an airplane, so he was excited about that, yet a little worried about the possibility of being airsick. He need not have worried,

perhaps due to his lack of eating, but he did not get sick.

Chapter 5

When Marty got off the plane in OKC, he looked around

and easily spotted Tim standing there waving at him. Marty

wore his old worn black hat and carried his small bag in

one hand, the other hand holding the saddle over his

shoulder. Tim led him to the escalators, then elbowed him

and winked. "Look out them stairs are moving," he said

and jumped back. He put his foot towards it, then jumped

back again. A guy in a business suit looked at them, then

walked past and got on the escalator. In Tim's truck later,

they had a good laugh at the expressions and stares of everyone in the metro airport.

Tim told Marty, "I have found a good club with plenty of young women to dance with. Are you game?"

"Hell yeah," Marty said.

They were on their way to Cattleman's in Waterton. Once there, Tim paid their way in and started a tab at the bar. They stayed and danced till last call for alcohol. Marty had told him that he didn't know when or how, he could pay him back for everything. Tim told him if he didn't have anything pressing, he could start work tomorrow morning. We have a little over a mile of fence that needs major repairs. It is through some rough timber on a lease we just got and we need it fixed so we can move cattle in.

"I can handle fence fixing as long as there is no snow or ice involved," proclaimed Marty.

They got to the hole in the wall at 3am, and Marty crashed on Tim's sofa. At 6am, the alarm was going off. Tim jumped up, showered, and started some coffee. He cooked some bacon and eggs, then they went to the lease. They worked all day cutting cedars for fence posts, then digging the holes and placing them. Just before dark, they quit for the day, cleaned up, and went back to the club. Two other old friends were there, and they all sat together at a large table right by the door to the restrooms. Marty saw a good-looking girl across from him and walked over to ask her to dance. She looked at him and told him to go away. He went back to his table and ordered a bloody Mary. He then folded a napkin just right and dipped the center into the drink. Then he walked past the girl, dropping the napkin at her feet as he passed. He circled around, then came back past her. "Ma'am, I think you lost something," he said as he walked away, with his back to her.

She looked down, seeing the napkin, and cussed at his back as he walked away. Tim watched this and was laughing as Marty sat back down. "I don't think you'll be dancing with her tonight," he said. "Let's order a beer."

After last call, they went home. Before 6am, Tim was yelling, "Up and at it, we're burning daylight." He was finished cooking breakfast and already dressed. They worked till dark on the fence. While taking a break and drinking water from the spring, they found some wild morel mushrooms. These they would fry for supper that night. The next morning was Monday, and Tim had to go to work at the electric company. He was a lineman and had a company truck. He drove it to work and left the keys to his personal truck with Marty. He worked all day on the fence. By the time Marty got back to Tim's house, he was home and cooking supper.

When the fence was completed, they worked the calves, then hauled all the cattle from the wheat pasture to the lease. Each load they hauled, they had to go through the town. There was some kind of festival going on with people everywhere. People were walking along the street as they went by, loaded down with cattle right off wheat pasture. Marty felt like he had paid Tim back for all he had done for him, said that he was going to look for work to pay for, bull riding entry fee. He wanted to get back to riding bulls again. He went to work with his brother Kevin and Carter for a while, but he didn't like the hours as it wouldn't allow him to go to many of the rodeos. He did earn enough to pay for, entry fee to a few rodeos.

Marty let everyone know he was going to enter the Arden Rodeo in a week. When the time came, he wasn't surprised to see most of his friends there. Kevin couldn't come as he was working away on the drilling rig. Billy and Cheryl did come to the rodeo, and Billy wanted to help pull the rope for him. Tim was there too, with Chelsea, his girlfriend. They had dated before but broken up after he had disappeared for two weeks. It turned out, though, that he had gone to work and then was called to leave the state to help repair power lines from tornado damage. Where he was working, there was no power or phones. She thought he had stood her up and wouldn't talk to him afterwards.

Marty rode his bull that night and invited everyone to go with him to a club in Melville. Billy and Cheryl went with him, but Tim took Chelsea home. At the club, Marty danced most of the night with the girl named Carly. At the end of the night, he went home with her. He spent the rest of the weekend with her. They went to the club again the next night, and he spent that night with her too. Sunday afternoon Marty called Tim to come pick him up. Tim came and took him to his mom and dad's trailer. Marty didn't have to go back to work till later in the week, but his mom told him he had to help out in the store.

The next week, Marty wasn't able to enter a rodeo, as he had to work on the drilling rig. The next weekend, though, he entered a rodeo, but was bucked off. Marty was building up his muscle tone, but in the wrong places for riding. This on again off again bull riding wasn't perfecting his skills. He was also losing girls as fast as he met them. Most of the time, the girls he met had found a new friend while he was working. The work was hard and long. He would work for twelve hours a day, hard strenuous labor for a full week. Their rig was now nearly a day away from home. They had a dog house to sleep in on their hours off, while the other shift worked. During the week they had off, two days were spent going either to or from the work site. That left five days off work. Usually, his mom had something for him to do much of that time. This didn't allow any time for riding bulls, or for girls. If he did meet a girl and told her he worked in the oilfield, she wouldn't talk to him anymore. Most of the girls didn't like roughnecks, seemed they had a bad reputation.

Fall came, and his friend Tim had planned a weekend party. It was on his weekend off, and there wasn't a rodeo. Tim would have a keg of beer and would tap it as soon as he got off work Friday evening. He invited them to all come over and party all weekend or till the keg went dry. He had ribs and brisket to BBQ on his grill. Billy told him that he and Cheryl were going to be there, but he had some things to do before he would arrive. Cheryl was working in the city and would stop by on her way home from work.

Marty walked across the highway to Tim's house from his mom's store. He was the first one there. He saw Tim's work truck parked in the back, so he knew he was there. Marty grabbed a red Solo cup and filled it out of the keg, then plopped himself down on the sofa and turned on the T.V. The keg was in a small horse tank filled with ice around the keg. Tim carried a bag of charcoal out to start the grill heating. Kevin came in while Tim was starting the charcoal. Derick came shortly later and filled a cup before sitting at the table. Tim was going to cook some burgers and hotdogs on the grill for tonight. He had buns, chips, and dip laid out on the countertop. Burgers and beer would make a good meal, as far as Marty was concerned. There were many times up on the mountain that he would have loved to have a burger with a cold beer. Though he was just getting to the point he didn't mind holding something cold in his hand.

Cheryl, Billy's wife, came in after that and told Tim she wanted to talk to him. They went down the hall to talk alone. Tim had left the doors open, and they stood in the back of the house talking. Cheryl told Tim that she had been involved with her photographer. She had told Billy, and he had started having an affair with a different woman. She thought that their marriage was over, and she didn't know what to do. He told her that Billy and she were great together and that if she was over her affair with the photographer, they should talk it out and stay together. If they could get beyond it, they should try. They had several years invested in their marriage, and both deserved to have a new start. While they were talking in the back, Tim noticed several others coming in the front door. Cheryl left after that, and returned a couple hours later, with Billy.

Marty and his friends played music, talked, and drank till late in the morning. Tim woke up a little after dawn and fixed some breakfast. He put the ribs on to smoke slow before he went to bed that night. Later he went across the street to get some more ice to put on the keg. Marty had got up and checked the ribs turning them. By midafternoon, everyone was there again, and they pulled the ribs out to eat. They ate all the ribs and again talked and drank till well after midnight.

Before going to sleep, Marty helped put the brisket on the smoker. Sunday afternoon, they ate the brisket, and by dark, had finished off the keg. Some of them had to go to work early the next morning. The first night Cheryl, and

Billy hadn't sat next to each other but, after that, they held each other all the time they were there. Nobody but Tim knew about their troubles, and he wasn't about to say anything, as far as he was concerned, it was their business. He was just glad to see them getting along so well. He thought Cheryl was very beautiful, and he really liked her, but Billy was a good friend.

On later weekends, Marty often went to the club with his brothers and friends. Some of the time, they would hook up with some women, sometimes not. On occasions, Billy and Cheryl would go with them. There were times that Tim would be there, and Cheryl would ask to dance with him. Tim would dance with her and talk, but would not hold her close. It wasn't because he didn't like her, but because he liked her too much. He didn't want to be the cause of any more problems between Billy and her.

Late in the winter, the entire group was at the club. They were celebrating Marty's birthday. He drank enough that, by the end of the night, he decided that he was going to ride one of the saddles hanging by a chain from the ceiling. These saddles were at the second-floor level, and to get to them, he had to climb over a railing and out onto a short rafter. From here, he jumped out onto the saddle. As this is as dangerous as it sounds, it was against all the clubs' rules. They even had a sign stating not to try it. The bouncers were on Marty soon after he got on the saddle and dragged him off. After this, he was barred from coming in the club again. "Oh well, there are plenty other clubs," he said. Later, he learned that the list only applied for that year, and he was again allowed in. The club had missed his friend's business, as about a dozen of them had stopped going there.

Chapter 6

Marty worked the summer and through the winter. He
rode in all the rodeos he could during that time. He also
dated several different women during that time. Late
winter, his father in Utah called him with a couple job
offers. Some cattlemen wanted a man to herd cattle up on
the mountain for the summer. He wasn't interested in going
back up on the mountain again. Then his dad told him that
a stock contractor was looking for a hand and gave Marty
his contact information. The stock contractor had a large

ranch in the valley, with hands working there and at the many rodeos he contracted for.

Marty called the stock contractor about the job. He was tired of the oil field. It wasn't for him. He liked the money and being off work for a week at a time, but he didn't like the work or the hours. A chance to work with a rodeo stock contractor sounded really good to him. Over the phone, they told him he could ride when he wanted to, and their ranch was in the valley in central Utah. He would work on the ranch as well as going to most of the rodeo's they contracted at. He would be one of three pickup men for bucking the rough stock, and he would be handling the bulls.

After packing his bags, Marty went to the bus stop. He was on his way to Utah, again. He had a large bag in one hand, and his saddle held over his right shoulder. No one paid much attention to him in this small Oklahoma town. When he got off the bus in Salt Lake City, though, he drew a sizable amount of attention. He wore cowboy boots with spurs, blue jeans, western shirt, and an old worn black hat. Tied on his saddle was a lariat rope, and his bag was a faded duffle. He was picked up at the door with a man in a cowboy hat holding a sign with his name. It was the foreman of the ranch.

On the ride out to the ranch, the foreman explained to Marty what was expected of him. He would stay in the bunk house with the other cowboys. The ranch was fifteen miles from the nearest town. When the work was done and there wasn't a rodeo, they would have Saturday night off in the town. The rodeo's that he went to, he had to work at. He would be allowed to enter and ride, but had to go right back to work after. The cowboys working with the stock contractors' job weren't done till the livestock had all been cared for. After that, he could go to any dance or celebration that was going on. He just had to be up bright eyed and bushy tailed at dawn to help feed the stock. He was also told that a movie studio was going to be filming near the ranch, and they would be providing the horses and other stock as needed. They would have him and the other cowboys take care of the livestock at the set.

They did film the movie, and during one scene, he and another cowboy were walking to the fire pit for a cup of coffee, when they were caught on film in the background. This weren't cut out, so Marty got to be in a movie, if only for a second. They did have to sign a release but wasn't paid any extra for it. Even with working at the movie set, this was what cowboy work was supposed to be, Marty thought. He did go to all the rodeos with the contractor. He also rode bulls in every event. He won a few, but not many. This was a higher level than he had been used to. These bulls were better than the ones he had rode in the past, too. This was pro rodeo, and the only ones he had rode in before were semi pro. The entry fees were higher too, but that also made the purses higher. One night, he won fifteen hundred dollars. For Marty, that was a load of cash. After buying a round for each of the other cowboys, though, it put a big dent in his earnings. Seemed like this was expected if he won big.

At one rodeo, the bullfighter did not show up. This left Marty's boss in a bind, as the bullfighter was an important part of the staff. Most people don't know that at a rodeo, there is a clown and a bullfighter. The clown is mostly what he looks like, but in a pinch, may help out the fighter. A bullfighter, though dressed like a clown, is there to protect the cowboy. He has to be fast on his feet and able to pivot and change directions on a dime. This way, he can run in front of the bull and turn beside him out of the bull's path. The foreman had watched Marty playing with the bulls in the pens at the ranch. He asked Marty if he thought he could be the bullfighter for this rodeo. "I'll give it a whirl," Marty said. This got him started in a short career fighting bulls at the rodeos.

Marty found that he was a good bullfighter. If a rider went down, he would rush in and draw the bull's attention away from the fallen cowboy. He quickly found that if girls loved bull riders, they adored bullfighters. He learned to leave a little of his makeup on after the rodeo to attack girls. One night, he picked up Debbie. She was gorgeous, with long light brown hair and blue eyes. She began following the rodeo circuit just to see him. They spent those weekends together, before the contractor would load up the stock and move on. Usually, they would return to the ranch and let the stock rest up for the next rodeo. The contractor started using Marty strictly for bullfighting at the rodeos. At the ranch, though, Marty still had regular cowboy chores to do. This included working cattle and helping with the round ups. He was no longer considered the new hand, though, and didn't have to muck out the stalls.

Back at the ranch, the owner talked to Marty, telling him they were done with rodeo for this season. They would have a job for him next spring if he wanted to come back. He could stay on if he wanted to ride line shack for the winter. He also told Marty that he had done so well fighting bulls that he had earned enough recognition to be rated number four in the circuit. This meant that he was in third standby for national finals. That didn't amount to a whole lot, though, as it was highly unlikely that he would be called in. Marty told him thanks, and he would probably be back next spring, but he wanted to go back to Oklahoma for the winter.

Before he left, though, he called Debbie, and she came to pick him up. They spent a few days together before she took him to the bus depot for his ride home. Marty had been on the bus overnight and was well aware that they were going down the highway past his mom's trailer and then the store. He moved up right behind the driver and asked if there was any way he could be put off at the store. He told the driver that it was his mother's place and he had been away for nearly a year.

The driver pulled over and helped him get his gear off the bus. His mother was in the store and saw him getting off the bus. She had wondered if the bus was having trouble when she saw it pull over. After a welcome home, his mother told him she had left his stepdad, Pop and that she was in the process of selling the store. She was living with her mom now about thirty miles away. He would go there with her after she closed for the night.

Marty said he would just go across the road and stay with Tim. She told him that Tim had gotten married and was living at his old house. His parents had bought a newer house and let him have the old one. Marty went home with his mother, but later stayed with Tim and Dolly. Tim and his dad hired Marty part of the time to help with the livestock. They had registered cattle and were showing the better ones at stock shows. They were selling some breeding stock and building a fair ranch. Their cattle were very large and, for the most part, gentle. The backs of the cattle were taller than his head. Tim said that didn't amount to much as he wasn't that tall anyway.

At the Tulsa State Fair, they were there with two heifers and a young bull for the open class show. On the second night there, Dolly came knocking at the hotel door. Tim and Dolly left but came back a couple hours later. She stayed the night and went back home the next morning. She came to tell Tim that she was pregnant. He told Tim that when they got back home, as soon as they unloaded, he should take him to his mother's trailer house. She had sold the store, bought a double wide trailer house, and had it set up on her mother's land.

Marty went to Tim's place during the finals rodeo to watch it on his big screen T.V. On the third night the bullfighter was hurt and had to be carried away to the ER.

The runner up was brought in for the rest of the rodeo. If this fighter got hurt Marty might be called to go and standby. That didn't happen, though and he only watched it on T.V.

Winter came and went with Marty working a few part time jobs. By spring. he was more or less broke. He picked up one more part time job for bus fare back to Utah. He got back to the ranch to find the owner had died, and the daughter had sold all the rodeo stock. The foreman hired him to work cattle for the summer, but the money wasn't nearly as good. Marty was spending most of his paycheck as fast as he was paid, as well as the rest of the cowboys. He wasn't able to get away much except for a few hours every other weekend or so. Seeing where this was going and that only the old hands would be kept on at the ranch for the winter; he decided to lay back some cash for bus fare back to Oklahoma.

As the days started getting shorter, they offered him a job for the winter up on the mountain. He wasn't about to spend another winter on the mountain, even if it was in a valley. He turned that down and caught a bus, back to Oklahoma. This time he rode the bus all the way to the station and called his mom to come get him.

He found out that Tim had a son and that Dolly had run off with a trucker while the baby was in the hospital. He remembered a night that he and Kevin were both at his house late at night, and she had come in cussing about them being there. He went into the kitchen to try to calm her down. They heard a commotion and looked into the kitchen. He saw Dolly pick up a butcher knife and go at Tim with it. As she raised the knife, Tim dropped and spun on one foot, low to the floor. He swung out the other leg hitting her behind her knees. She fell backwards, as he slapped the floor with both hands and rolled over and up to a squat. Then he was on top of her. He had a knee on her wrist that held the knife. Both his feet were on her legs, pinning them. His other arm was wrapped around her free arm, with his wrist on her throat. After a little bit, she said, "You can let me go now."

She told him that she deserved that, and she was leaving for good though. He could keep his bastard son, and always wonder who's boy he really was.

After she had left, Marty said "That's the craziest thing I ever saw. I never knew you could fight like that."

"I've had some training by a military hand to hand combat instructor," Tim said.

A few days later, Marty had come back over to see Tim. Neither he nor Kevin wanted to hang around too much, as Tim might want them to babysit while he was at work. He talked to Tim about going back to rodeoing around locally. He was going to get what he could fighting bulls or riding. Tim told him that he used to ride bareback and some saddle bronc, but it had been a while. They decided to get ready and go in together.

Together they signed up for a nearby rodeo the next weekend. They left right after Tim got home from work that afternoon. Tim was signed up for bareback riding and Marty bull riding. Bareback riding is always first, in the lineup. He had brought his son Jason along, and as they were walking around, the barrel racers were all hanging out around them. The girls were oohing and aahing with the baby. They asked the girls if they would mind watching the boy while Tim rode his bronc. They were happy to accommodate. "This might be a rewarding arrangement, Tim" Marty said.

"I noticed," Tim answered, smiling. Tim got bucked off, but Marty rode his bull. The next week was another rodeo. It went much the same way, with Tim getting bucked off and Marty riding his bull for the money. A week later, they were at a bigger rodeo, and they got the same girls to watch after Jason while Tim rode. This time he rode and was in the money. Marty, though, drew a bull called Buzzsaw. He was thrown hard. On the way home, Marty said he thought he might have broken his wrist or arm. He wouldn't go to the ER, though. Tim asked about next week. "We have already paid up for it, and you know you can't get your money back. You'll just lose it if you don't ride."

"What if I draw that same bull again?" Marty asked.

"How much chance do you think there is of that happening? There is no way you will draw the same bull two weekends in a row."

"Near impossible. I think I could do alright as long as I don't draw that same bull," said Marty.

The next week, they went to the rodeo. Marty had wrapped his wrist and lower arm tight as he could. They went up to the van to draw for their rides, and Marty drew Buzzsaw again. "Damn," he said. "I'm just going to tell them to let that damn bull go." He went ahead and got ready for his ride, though.

Tim rode his bronc, but it hardly bucked. The contractor offered him a reride after the regular rodeo, but Tim refused. He could already tell that Marty wasn't into this rematch with Buzzsaw. Sure, enough, barely out of the chutes, Marty was bucked off and went down hard again. Still, he wouldn't go to the ER. Marty did go to the doctor the next day, and his arm was broken. He would be in a cast for a couple months, if not more. Most of the rest of this rodeo season would be over before his arm would be out of a cast. Even then it would take a couple more months to build his strength back up in his arm for riding.

Marty had a little money saved up and picked up a few odd jobs. He started going to a club up in the big city. Here he met a girl that was interested in him. He told her about busting his arm riding bulls, and she was fascinated by that. She had dated some would be cowboys, but Marty seemed to be the real thing. Her name was Rose, she had three kids,

which Marty got to know, and they adored him.

Chapter 7

Marty had his arm out of the cast and was hanging out at his mom's place. Kevin was there too, as was his sister. It was winter and near freezing when a storm moved in. Lightning struck nearby with a loud clap of thunder. Then the sky opened with hard rain. The heavy rain continued all night and into the next day. Their lights went out shortly after the rain had started, and they had lit some candles to see by. Marty had bundled up in a blanket on the sofa, but was awakened several times during the night by loud cracking and crashing sounds. A couple times the trailer house rocked.

The next morning, he woke up cold and hungry. They still had no power. They had a small propane heater that helped some. He looked outside, and all the trees around the trailer were broken. Every limb was hanging and covered with a heavy thick layer of ice. The barbed wire fence was covered in the ice and drooped under the weight. As far as he could see, everything was coated with a thick layer of the crystal looking ice. They ate some cereal with what milk was left for breakfast. His mom had already called the electric company about being out and was told they were working on it. The lady had also told her that they had thousands of outages across the system, and it might be days or weeks. before they could get it all on.

Later that day while they were all bundled up together in the living room, they heard a truck pulling in. Tim knocked on the door. He was there with his work truck. "Marty, I

have a job for you, if you're interested in going to work."
Marty jumped up, grabbing his coat and hat. "You might
want to pack a bag. It may be a week or two before we get
off and you can come back here," Tim advised. "If you got
warm clothes and leather gloves you will need them along
with a spare pair of work boots."

They went right to work on a line several miles away.
Marty had asked if they were going to get his mom on and
was told the power wasn't even on to that substation. They
would have to wait till the generation and transmission
company restored that before they could work on her line.
They worked all afternoon with only one break, when a
pickup from the company pulled up where they were, with
some pop and sandwiches. After working all night, they
went to the electric company's office a couple hours before
dawn. Tim told him to fill the truck with fuel, and by that
time he would have the equipment they needed piled up in
the warehouse on the floor.

Once they had everything, they needed loaded, they went into the office and to the linemen's room. Ladies from the office had a hot meal laid out for them and many other linemen. As soon as Marty had finished eating, he was told to go fill out some paperwork so he could get paid come payday. He finished his paperwork, and they were going back out to work. The two of them were being assigned to lines that didn't have any broken poles. They were cutting trees and pulling up line, to get each tap ready to restore power. If they did find a broke pole, they called it in for a crew with a pole truck.

On one three phase junction pole, Tim had climbed to the top. It was getting dark as he had started up the pole. Marty pulled up a broken wire to him on a handline. Tim had a belt hoist, which he caught off the line and was pulling it into sag. Marty was standing around, watching him, wondering what he could do to help. He heard Tim grunting and asked, "do you need something?"

"Just another hand," Tim said. Feeling the pole rock, Tim looked down the pole to see Marty trying to bear hug the pole and climb it. "No, don't be trying to get up here. I can get it. You're not trained and don't have the gear to climb a pole." They finally got that line up and were a mile down the road at the fuse feeding that tap. They removed the ground chains and were waiting for radio time to call in for permission to energize the tap. After getting that line on, they were told they could go home and sign off for some sleep till an hour before sunrise.

They went together to Tim's house and went to sleep. They were up early and back to the office before dawn. Again, the ladies had a hot meal for them. Marty filled the truck with gas and loaded the material while Tim got orders as to where they were working that day. Smiling, Tim hopped in the truck and they went back to his house. He lived on a short tap and was the only house that was out on that line. Since there was one tree that had broken and laid

115

across the line, they were going to get it on first. When they got off next time, they would have a nice warm place to sleep and would be able to take a shower. You just don't know how good a hot shower is, until you have had to work hard for a couple weeks in the cold, without one.

Marty had been told by several now, that if he continued to work like he was, he might be able to get a full-time job. He liked the work and the feeling of a sense of pride, when they got a line on. Most people came out and showed appreciation when their power was restored. There were some days that they worked with a contract crew. They would show them where poles were broken and leave them working on them, while they put up some line or drove out other lines that hadn't been looked at yet. They would return to the contract crews after a couple hours to see how they were doing. After six weeks of working thirty-six hours plus before a break, they began getting every night off. They would get off at ten PM or midnight. They were required to be back to the office an hour before dawn each morning.

For two more weeks, they worked getting most of the power back on to the homes. They still had a lot of line and poles down feeding water wells, fence chargers, and oil wells. At this point, though, they were allowed to take off Sundays. That Saturday night, they got off work at nine PM and went to the Cattleman's night club. They ate a steak there, before dancing with the girls and drinking their fill of beer. Marty slept till noon Sunday, then ate a big lunch. They lay around the house and watched T.V, before going to sleep, they had to be at work early the next morning.

Monday morning, Marty was back to the company office an hour and a half before dawn. Marty had learned to fill the truck with fuel and load all the material they used the day before. He was with Tim and they went to work on a long line that went across country to wells. This line had no poles broken so they were clearing trees and putting lines back up. Since he had started, everyone that had worked with him had told him what each piece of equipment was called, what it was used for, and how it worked. Marty had caught on fast to the work. Now Tim was talking him through the use of an extendo stick. It was a fiberglass stick just over four feet tall that could extend up to forty feet. It had a hook on the end which could be used to fuse a line or open them up to work on.

After all the houses had been restored with electricity, the contractors had been let go. Now that they were finishing getting all the power restored, Marty was being kept on, at least till all the cleanup was done. A month later, all the local hands that had been given a part time job were let go, with the thanks of the company. All but Marty, he was hired as a full-time employee. He was then placed on a construction crew, thereby, he would not be working with Tim anymore. He was now working on a crew that was putting up new poles and line each day. The guys told him that in a year or two, he might get the chance to become an apprentice lineman. It would then take at least four more years to complete training to become a journeyman lineman. At each step along the way, he would receive a pay increase. He would have to learn from a book as well as the on-the-job training and pass a test at each step.

Marty bought a new pickup, the first he had ever owned. With a fulltime job, he was able to finance it. He needed his own transportation to get to work. At a local rodeo, he rode a bull and won some money. He also hooked up with an old girlfriend, Brenda. He spent the weekend with her. He also got a job for the next weekend fighting bulls at a rodeo.

Marty always showed up for work early and stayed till time to sign off. Every time he was called after hours to work, he jumped up and went. The overtime pay was really good. Many times, when Tim was called out, he asked for Marty to go with him. This one time they went to work together; they pulled up on a blown fuse. It was a Sunday afternoon, and there had been a heavy rain which had come through that area.

They found the blown fuse on a stepdown transformer bank. Marty was told to get the fuse barrel down and ready to refuse. He pulled the barrel down with the extendo stick and was surprised to find a large eighty-amp fuse. The copper braid wire coming out of it was the largest he had ever seen. After getting clearance from the office to try it, Marty put it in. As fast as he shoved it in, the transformers started jumping up and down with a loud roar. Fire engulfed the area around the fuse barrel, and an explosion like a canon roared. Marty could feel the hot air, melted bits of copper, and pressure from the blowing fuse as he dropped the extendo stick and ran around the truck. "What the hell was that?" he yelled.

"The fuse blew. Now we have to find the problem on the line," stated Tim between fits of laughter.

Tim drove them straight to a man hole in a housing addition along a creek. They opened it up to find it filled with water. They got a battery-operated sump pump out of a tool bin and pumped water out. As the water receded, Marty could see a pole type transformer in the hole. The water had covered the open bushings and connections of both the primary and secondary. While the pump was working, Marty said, "You knew this was here, didn't you?" Once they had finished pumping the water all out, they went back to the fuse. Tim told him to get ready to try the fuse again while he called in for clearance to try it. Before shoving it in, he looked back to see Tim sitting in the truck, with his hands covering his ears. This time, Marty held his breath as he tried it. With a sigh of relief, he put the stick up after closing the fuse in, restoring power to the housing addition. From the hillside, they looked down toward the creek bottom watching the lights all come on.

That fall, Tim asked Marty if they could find a place to hunt mule deer up in Utah. Marty told him sure they could hunt on the mountain that he had spent the winter on. It was a good place with plenty of mule deer. Marty, Tim, and Tim's dad all went together for a long weekend hunting trip. They drove straight through, taking turns driving. They bought their out of state hunting license and went to Marty's dad's house. Ryan, Marty's dad, was going to take them up on the mountain and show them where to go. He was also taking two of his horse's up there for them to use.

As they got to the line shack, Ryan watched while the others set up camp. He put the horses in the stall and turned back to see Tim hanging up a trash bag. He had already fixed a latrine downstream from the camp. Smiling, he decided that he liked these guys and the way they operated. A little later, they were cooking supper over a blazing fire and asked if he would like to stay and eat with them. He told them he would stay the night, but he had to be back down the mountain before dark tomorrow night.

Before dark, Tim and Marty had gone out scouting and looking for deer. They only had a buck license. They had seen several does, but so far, no bucks. They had walked to the large deep canyon and down into it. They walked a mile down the canyon, but as it started getting dark, they had trouble finding a path up out of the steep canyon walls. As they were walking earlier, they had spotted a mountain lion pacing them from a ledge overhead. Tim had pointed his rifle at the lion, but Marty told him not to shoot it unless it attacked them. The mountain lions were not in season and were reserved for resident hunters only.

An hour later, they could smell the smoke from camp and turned back. Ryan had told them there was a rock fall that had a trail next to it. Billy had used it before. They saw the rock fall, but no trail. There were fresh rocks that had fallen, and they figured the rocks covered the trail. Some of

these rocks were bigger than a cabin. They made it back to
the place they had come down and were able to climb back
up at that location. They had to sling their rifles on their
backs and climb on all fours as the loose dirt and pebbles
made climbing rough. It was nearly midnight when they
walked back into camp. Food and a warm bed were waiting
for them with hot coffee. Sitting around the fire eating,
Tim's dad said he knew they would find their way back
eventually. Marty's dad wasn't so sure. All in all, they had
a good hunt and took plenty of meat back home with them.
Tim's dad wasn't' sure he was going to be able to handle
the mountain air as he had suffered lung cancer and had
half his left lung removed. He didn't have any trouble
though and thoroughly enjoyed himself. This trip reminded
him of his younger years, when he would go hunting out of
state with his brothers and father. His dad had died a few
years earlier, but this trip with his son and friend seemed to
ease his heart. Marty had become like another son to him

and Tim's mom. Since he had started work at the electric company with Tim, Marty sometimes stayed with them.

After their vacation, most of the weekends, Marty now spent with Brenda. She even went to the rodeos with him. He was fighting bulls more than riding them now. After a few months, he asked her to marry him. They were married a month later and rented a small house on the edge of town. Things were going pretty well; till one Friday night he went to a rodeo up by the city. Brenda went to her family for her mother's birthday. After the rodeo, Marty went to the club in the city. He saw Rose there, and they danced till closing. Unknown to Marty, a friend of Brenda was there and saw him leave with Rose. Marty returned home around four am to find Brenda's things all gone and a note saying she knew about what happened in the city, and she was filing for a divorce.

Marty let the rent house go and signed the divorce papers when they came to him. For several weeks he worked hard every day and either went to a rodeo or the club. There was a tornado on Memorial Day weekend. It hit just before five o'clock on Friday afternoon. Before anyone had signed off for the day, the boss came around, saying, "hold up boys, we may need everyone to work overtime. It looks like a big tornado, and outages are starting to come in already. Get your gear already and stock up with extra supplies." The tornado left over a half mile wide path that went on for twelve miles on the ground. It took out several homes and miles of power lines and poles.

They worked through till nearly dark Sunday night. Around noon Saturday, the Red Cross set up a disaster relief van right near where they were working. A representative talked to the foreman, telling them to come by and eat anytime they had a chance and eat all they wanted. They worked hard day in and day out, rebuilding the lines. One house that was destroyed had moved in a RV. They helped the people unhook the house and attach the RV. The work went on till late Sunday afternoon, when they turned on the last line. By that time, they had everyone back on, but they were worn out. He went to his stepdads to sleep, and all the other linemen went to their homes to sleep. There was a little clean up the next week, but not nearly as bad as the ice storm had been. Forty-eight hours from the time the tornado hit, they had everyone's power back on. They had changed out thirty-four poles and put-up miles of line. On Saturday afternoon, a news helicopter orbited overhead as they were working. Once they were home family members talked about seeing some of them on the news.

An area lineman quit to go to another company, and a journeyman moved up. This left an opening for an apprentice. Marty got that job. Along with it, he received a set of belt and hooks. He had tried climbing before and did well with it. Climbing a pole with a belt and hooks was tough on a person's feet and knees, but he got used to it soon enough. With this new job, came a really good raise.

He felt good about himself, and this was the longest he had

ever worked at the same job. He could see himself working

here till he retired. He felt like he fit in and was happy.

The next weekend, he went to the city and the club. He

spotted Rose and went to her table. He danced with her and

talked till late. He suggested that they meet there again the

next night. Saturday night at the club, Marty was with Rose

again. After a few beers and dancing, she told him that he

could spend the night at her apartment if he chose. "Sure,

sounds like a great idea to me," he said. She told him that

he needed her every day, and if he wanted, he could move

in with her. He was staying at his stepfather's during the

week and his moms on the weekends. He didn't have a

place of his own. Marty decided to give it a try, and the

next evening he brought all his belongings over to her

apartment. Her apartment was in the city and on the far side

from the office he worked out of.

Chapter 8

Marty lived in Rose's apartment with her for two weeks. She had learned that he was paid bimonthly and when those paychecks came in. By his next payday, she had convinced him to turn it over to her to help with bills and to put some away for savings. He never liked taking care of bills and often forgot to pay them on time, so this seemed like a good idea. The company discovered that it took so long for him to drive there and was no longer calling him regularly for outages. This cut back on his overtime pay.

Work each weekday started at eight am. Marty was there at least fifteen to thirty minutes early each day. This required him to leave Rose's apartment between six am and six fifteen. If he got off work on time, he didn't get back to the apartment till six thirty each evening. She would give him enough money for his lunch and to buy his tobacco each day. The rest of his money, she told him, went to bills and to a savings account.

The crew Marty worked on was assigned a long three phase conversion job. They were on a time frame to complete the job. They began working till dusk each day. This caused Marty to arrive home late each day. Some days it was nine or ten pm, and he had to leave for work now around four am. Rose became suspicious and checked up on him. Sure enough, he was working late and by his next pay check the extra hours showed as overtime pay. Rose started spending more time around Marty's hometown looking for a house to rent.

Once Rose found a large nice house that she loved, she started manipulating Marty toward marriage. She waited for a night that Marty came home from work very late and tired. She then told him about the house and that it was only four miles from his company's office. He wouldn't have to drive so tired when he had to work late. He would also be more available for afterhours service calls. She then told him they wouldn't be able to get the house as single adults living together. The owners were very provincial and only would rent to a married couple. He said, "Let's get married then." She filled out the paperwork, and they were married at the courthouse not long after.

They moved into the very nice large house with her children. Things seemed to be going great for them, though she continued to give him just enough money for lunch and his tobacco. He had received three more raises and was near making journeyman lineman. He now was getting called regular for outages calls. They liked him near, as he would always answer and come right away. The lineman didn't have to wait for him to show up. Many times, he would be there before the lineman and have any special equipment they might need ready.

A late-night storm had come through, causing some damage. Marty was called into work along with as many other linemen as were available. The crew Marty was working on had replaced three broken poles on a main three phase feeder. He was on the junction pole to pull in the lines that had broken. He was sitting on the top crossarm beam, placing a hoist on the broke phase when someone shouted, "Get clear someone is heating the line up." Marty swung himself under the crossarm beam, holding on only by his hands. He looked down and let go. He had swung himself to the uphill side of the pole, and by hanging on to the cross arm, he was only twenty-two feet from the ground. He dropped free and clear with no injury.

Once he had shaken off the fall and scare of the line, being energized, he demanded to know who had turned it on. "Why the hell did they heat up the line I was working on?" he yelled. Before he had jumped, a man with his crew had picked up the radio mic, yelling, don't energize men working on the line. Hearing this, the dispatcher had called all crews to stop work immediately. It was a near miss, and no one was hurt. No more work was done until the supervisors had been called in and arrived at the work sites. After they had determined what had happened and why, they watched carefully as the work was completed and all lines reenergized safely. Once they were cleared to go back to work, the foreman asked Marty if he was willing to go back up that pole and finish his work. He told him not really, but it would probably be best if I did it myself. He climbed back up the pole and placed extra grounds on the line before he would touch it. He finished his work and came down with a sigh.

The next day at work, though, they all talked over what had happened, why, and what should be done to prevent it happening again. As it turned out, the crew who energized the line had been working on a different circuit coming from the same substation and intended to energize that circuit. The switches were marked wrong. Most stations were marked numbering from left to right, this one, though, was numbered right to left. That system was changed, and every switching system from then on was numbered left to right. Not long after, grounds were required to be placed within sight of the men working instead of at the opened point. Many of the men had known other linemen that had died in similar circumstances. This time, Marty was lucky. Marty and several others that night learned that to live as a lineman, you had to depend not only on luck, but safe work practices. Eventually, all work had to be done with grounds on both sides of the work; in sight of the workers. They also had to have a tag with the lineman's name at the location of the open switch and locked to it. Only that lineman was to remove the tag, and only that lineman had the key.

Marty and Rose were invited to be the witnesses for Tim and Chelsea's wedding. Jason and them were the only ones there other than the preacher. It was in a church, and Marty told the preacher he was surprised the ceiling didn't fall in on them. He had never been inside of a church. Jason was five and held the rings in the ring box. He was opening the box and snapping the top closed with a loud pop. Marty reached down and held his hand, and the box closed.

Later, Tim transferred to the south east district, and they found a house with some acreage for sale. Marty, Billy, and Derick helped them move. Tim would now have a one-man basket truck to work in and wouldn't have to climb poles anymore. He would be working in this district and, most of the time, not going to any other areas served by the company. His home was twenty-five miles from the office and Marty's house. He would see his friend on occasion, but not very often. Tim also did everything in his power to stay away from the office. He had said it was too much like politics around that office.

On a Friday afternoon, they were getting off work on time. Several of the guys were talking about going to the city to a strip club, to celebrate finishing another big job. Marty told them he couldn't, and besides he didn't have any money. They told him to come on and they would comp him. It had been a long time since he had gone out with the guys, so he went. While they were out, Rose called the dispatcher asking when Marty would get off work. The dispatcher told her he had gotten off on time that afternoon. Rose was up waiting on him when he got home at three am drunk. She chewed him out and made him sleep on the lawn outside the house. The next week, she didn't give him any tobacco or lunch money. He thought to himself, *This flower I married has thorns. Rose is a fitting name in more*

ways than one.

After a few days, she calmed down some, but was still very jealous of Marty's every minute. Marty worked each day and returned home directly after work. No more did he go out for a drink with the guys. He got another promotion and was highly thought of at work for his work ethics. He always joked around with the guys, but wouldn't stop for a drink after work with them anymore. As far as work was concerned, he seemed to be doing very well, till one Monday morning.

As Marty entered the lineman's room, some of the guys were reading the morning paper and looked up at him, whispering. Shortly later, he was called into the directors' office. He was asked if he had spent the weekend in jail. He said, "No, I was home with my wife all weekend." The director showed him the paper with an article saying he had been arrested for DUI and was in jail. He was told if it was him, he needed to straighten it out, and if he turned himself in for rehab his job would be waiting for him when he returned. "It wasn't me, though," he said.

"You need to get this straightened out as soon as you can then," the director said. "You will be off work till you do."

Marty went right home and told Rose all about it and what he had been told. She went with him to the jail to learn why and what had happened. At the jail, he showed them his license with his name and asked why they had said he was in jail. They escorted him back to a cell they said he was in. There, looking sick and disgusting, was his brother Kevin. With the jailer and a deputy standing by, Kevin admitted that he had told them his name was Marty and not Kevin. Marty and Rose got a confirmation to that fact, in writing and Marty took it to the director a few hours later. He was cleared and put back to work. Kevin, being Marty's brother, not only knew his name, but also his birthday and social security number. He had told the police this, trying to keep his name clear. Once he got out, though, it didn't matter to the oil field drilling company he worked for. It would have cost Marty his job though, he was required to have a class A CDL, and due to strict safety regulation in the electric industry, linemen could not have a DUI on their record.

Not long after that, Kevin was working on a drilling rig, when a piece of equipment fell and crushed his leg. He was taken to the ER but he lost his right leg. He spent two years in and out of the hospital and rehab. He was fitted with a prosthesis, but it took a long time for him to fully recover. While he was out of work, he did study and took the test to get his GED. Later, he got a job again with the same drilling company as a company man. He looked over three drilling rigs. After that, he was transferred to Utah and had rigs from Idaho to Colorado to watch.

Marty heard from another old friend about that time, Tony had gotten a job with the Texas State Troopers. He was there to visit his family and then came by to see Marty and Rose. Tony felt like things didn't seem to be right while he was with Marty and his wife. She was friendly enough, but something was wrong. He wasn't sure if it was his training or if there truly was something wrong. *Hopefully it would work itself out,* he thought to himself. Still, he just didn't like her.

Marty was helping with a new apprentice on the crew now. When he was called out to go on an after-hours outage, he took along his belt and hooks. Many of those afterhours calls, he would climb the pole while the journeyman watched over him. He hadn't missed any days and had worked hard. One day, while he was at work, Rose picked up the mail as usual. This day, there was a letter addressed to Marty from a Debbie in Utah. She knew Marty had been with many girls through the years, but this letter made her see red.

With fire in her eyes, Rose opened the letter to Marty from Debbie. What was he doing getting a letter from another woman? She ripped open the letter and began to read. This woman claimed to have a five-year-old daughter and claimed it was his. Rose had only been married to Marty just under three years. This Debbie went on to say that she might be dying and that Marty would have to take care of his daughter, if she did. She then said that she had HIV and that Marty might ought to get himself checked. Rose was furious. When Marty came home that afternoon, she confronted him about it. He didn't know anything about it and had no idea the girl might have been pregnant. He had spent some time with her years before and guessed it could be possible that he might be the father. This just made Rose even madder. "You may have HIV and may have infected me You ass hole," she yelled. "You are nothing but a womanizing bastard."

When Marty went to work the next day, she started planning on getting away from him. She knew he had a large life insurance; it was also his pension plan. It would pay three times his annual salary in case of death, to his family. A divorce would do away with her as a beneficiary and as none of her children were his, they wouldn't get anything either. This girl in Utah, though, could get it all. What was she to do, and how could she get the money. One thing she knew, she wanted to be away from him. She would not let him touch her ever again. As far as she was concerned, he was the scum of the Earth.

She went to the restaurant for lunch that she often hung out at during the day. Troy, the deputy, was there again, and as usual, he was hitting on her. This time, she encouraged him. He sat down with her and they began to talk. He knew she was married, but that didn't seem to bother him. Rose began to come up with a plan. She told the deputy that her husband was a drunken ass hole, that she needed to get away from. He acted sympathetic and touched her hand. She unbuttoned the top button on her blouse. She then looked at him, knowing she had him hooked. She raised her other hand to his face touching him lightly smiling. "Perhaps I should follow you home to be certain that you are okay," he suggested.

"That would be nice," she said smiling, and batted her eyes.

Rose drove her car home, with the deputy following behind her. She almost got sick thinking of the deputy and what she was about to do. At her house, she asked if he would check inside to make sure no one was there. He smiled and went inside, with her following close behind. Inside, he turned toward her and she placed her arms around him. After a couple weeks of them sleeping together during the day and Rose telling the deputy about Marty, they devised a plan. The people that had bought Marty's Mom's store had converted it into a bar, and that was a part of the plan. She started giving Marty a little extra cash on certain evenings, telling him he should stop for a beer or two before coming home from work. Due to the way she was treating him anymore, he was happy to stop off for a beer before going home.

The plan was made, and the trap was laid. Troy, the deputy, was also in on her plan. Now she just had to lure him into the trap and spring the snare. The deputy by now, was so involved that his ethics had been totally corrupted. He was now advising Rose how to do what she wanted. He had also volunteered to help her in the plan.

The day came that Rose gave Marty enough money for four or five beers. She had told him she was going to be late as she would be at a ballgame with her son. Marty stopped at the bar, which was only two miles from his house. Only one mile on the highway, the other down a dirt road. He drank four beers then left to go home. As soon as he pulled out onto the highway, red and blue lights began flashing in his rear-view mirror. He pulled over, and the deputy gave him a sobriety test. He failed and was handcuffed. The deputy left with him in the back seat. Marty was taken to the county jail.

In the drunk tank, he remembered what he was told when Kevin was in jail. Marty asked if he could be sent to rehab and told yes. He was taken to an alcohol rehab center for two weeks. While he was in the center, Rose filled for a restraining order against him. Three days into the rehab, Marty received a copy of the restraining order requiring him to stay at least a thousand yards away from Rose and her children.

Marty had no idea what was going on or why she would have placed this restraining order against him. He was devastated and furious. In his anger, he acted out against the faculty. He was then given another week, causing him to be in there for a total of three weeks. Not only was he angry, but also confused. He had a good job and was proud of the work he was doing. He had a good family, he had thought. Why was all this happening to him? He wasn't a bad person. He would share anything he had to help someone. What had caused all this to happen? More important, what could he do to get it all right again.

While Marty was in the rehab, Troy had been seeing Rose two or three times a week. He would spend a couple hours each time in her bed. On these days, her children were away to school. It didn't escape her that he was married and that he knew she was too. Neither seemed to care about that, though. She really didn't care about Troy in the least, at first, he even repulsed her. Now though, he was a means to an end. She would use him to get what she wanted, then drop him like the manure he was. She would screw anyone over to get what she wanted.

Troy didn't care that Rose was married. She was as good in bed as he had originally surmised. Her red hair was no joke, she felt ten degrees warmer than any other woman he had been with. Red heads had an insatiable warmth that drove him mad with lust. He was so obsessed with her now, that he would do anything for her. Case in point was him showing up at her home while he was on duty. He just didn't care about anything anymore, except his time with her. He was so obsessed now that he would do anything that she asked of him.

Everything that Marty owned was still in its place in their house. Rose was well aware of this, but wasn't going to do anything about it, yet. This too was a part of her plan. When the time was right, she would use his stuff to fulfill her plan. Her three children asked about Marty and what had happened. She did not tell them the truth, just that he had gotten into trouble and was away for the time. She didn't even tell them that she had a restraining order against him. They thought that their mom and Marty were getting a divorce, but that was the last thing she wanted, as she would lose any claim to his money. She had gotten used to using the majority of his pay checks. She had only let him

have a small fraction of each check. He didn't even know

how much money she was spending or where it went. The

last two checks she had cashed and had hidden on her

person. She might need all the cash she could get.

Chapter 9

Troy, the deputy, called Rose at three o'clock on a Friday
afternoon. Marty was released from the rehab. His mom
had picked him up and they were going to a lawyer. She
needed to get something done before his lawyer was able to
file any papers on Monday morning. He told her that it was
too late in the day for any paper to be filled then, so it
would be Monday morning before they could get them to
the court house. Rose couldn't allow Marty to file for a
divorce, it would complicate her getting his money. She
called Marty's mom later to talk to him, but found out that
he had left there. She then called his step dad's trailer, and

was told he hadn't seen him. Rose called her sister to come and get her children, asking if she could keep them till Sunday. She knew that her sister would, as Rose had kept her two children several times before. Whatever she was going to do, it had to be this weekend, and she didn't want her children around at that time.

Marty, after talking to a lawyer with his mom, went by Tim's house. Tim told him to be cool and follow his lawyer's advise. He told Tim that his lawyer was going to file for a divorce Monday morning as soon as the court house opened. He had been advised not to go anywhere near Rose or her children as long as she had a restraining order on him. Marty left there and went by Tim's mom and dad's house. They told him they would help anyway they could and that he needed to get with the electric company first thing Monday. He told them that he had called the company from his mom's house and was told his job was waiting for him. They had placed him on vacation time and he still had some time off left. He told them he would be at work Monday morning. They offered to let him stay with them, but he told them he would stay with his stepdad. Later Marty went to his stepdads for the weekend and to be ready to go to work Monday morning.

At midnight, Rose again called Marty's stepdad. Marty was there. The deputy had just left her house and was watching from just over the hill with his lights off. She told Marty that she was going to place all his belongings out on the yard, and he needed to come get them right then. The deputy had suggested this as a way to get him there late at night and in violation to the restraining order. Marty went to the house half dressed, as he had already been in bed asleep. He had hardly any clothes, as all he owned was in the house with Rose, including his last two pay checks. She had told him she had the checks, holding them for him. His stepdad's place was only a mile and a half away and all down a dirt road.

Marty got there to find all his clothes on the lawn, tossed every which way. He began gathering them up and putting them in his truck. He found his work clothes, his personal items, but not his rodeo gear, or his paychecks. He yelled in about his gear and money, Rose opened the garage door. He could see the door on into the house was open. She told him his gear was too heavy for her and was still on the floor of the closet; he was welcome to go in after it. He went in and through the house, with Rose following him. Marty opened the closet and picked up his rodeo gear bag. She told him his checks were on the night stand by the bed. He stood up and turned to see Rose pointing his twenty-two rifle at him. "You, sorry son of a bitch, die in hell!" she said as she squeezed the trigger. She shot him three more times before casually putting the rifle on the bed. She sat by it and waited, watching him. His head and shoulders twitched a couple times slightly. After that, he never moved again. For over thirty minutes, she watched to see if he would try to get up or if he was dead. She could see his chest still rise slowly with each breath. Nearly forty minutes later, Marty not having moved, she picked up the phone.

One bullet tore through the intestines and lodged in his spine. The other three bullets tore intestines and caused massive internal bleeding. Marty lay there in his own blood, slowly dying, yet fully aware of what was going on around him. He felt cold, though, and wondered at that. He knew he shouldn't have come here, and not inside. He remembered the lawyer telling him not to come here. He watched as she made a call, thinking she would call for an ambulance. He wondered why she had sat on the bed watching him for so long before calling for help. He was determined to make it till someone arrived. Instead, he heard her saying it was over. She then called 911 and told them she had shot her husband, that she had a restraining order against. She told them she had to protect herself as he tried to rape her. She was still on the phone with the operator when a deputy came into the room. It was the same one that had arrested him for DUI, and he was sure that he had seen him before. Then he saw Rose hug and kiss the deputy passionately. When they stopped, he heard the deputy say, "It will go down as justifiable homicide." At this point, Marty knew there was no help for him, and he slipped away.

The next morning, the sheriff's report went through, just like the deputy said, as justifiable homicide. Rose had requested that the body be sent off for cremation. She had already asked for the death certificate, she needed that. The county had no coroner, so the body had been held at the local hospital. They normally did so till funeral arrangements had been made, so they were only waiting for the crematorium van to arrive.

Marty's mother, upon hearing about him and what was happening, called the state attorney general. He called the

county and demanded that the body be sent to the city for
an autopsy. Three hours later, a van picked up Marty's
body and took it to a laboratory in the city.

Troy came into the sheriff's office later that afternoon.
He heard that the body had been moved to the city for an
autopsy. He became very moody and standoffish. He did
his paperwork there, reporting what he and Rose had
agreed on saying. He left to go see her again. At her house,
he told her that Marty wasn't being cremated right away
and indeed was going to the best labs in the state for an
autopsy. They were both concerned. She told him that he
should probably stay away from her for some time. What
she didn't tell him, though, was that she never wanted to
see him again.

Before the deputy had come to her house, Rose had found
the papers for Marty's life insurance and called the number.
She told them that he was dead and she was his sole
beneficiary. She was told she would need the death

certificate when they came to see her and before they could pay her. The next day, an investigative agent came by the electric company and asked a few questions. He went from there to Tim's mom and dad's house, looking for directions and information. The company had that address as an alternative address for Marty. Here he was told about the circumstances of his death, and that there were many questions as to those circumstances. With this information, the agent determined that there would not be any payment without much more investigation. He then went to the county sheriff's office and wasn't satisfied with the answers he received there. He was also concerned that they had a death certificate when an ordered autopsy had not been completed yet. That was against protocol.

When the agent went to see Rose at her house and told her this, she nearly went ballistic. This only confirmed the agent's summations about the probable cause. That night as, Rose lay down to sleep, she was awakened by four shots outside. This happened again the next night, and the next. Each time it was around twelve thirty am, the time she had shot Marty. She was now certain that Marty's brothers and or friends were trying to send her a message. She didn't think anyone knew, about her first husband having died too. As far as anyone knew, he slowly got sick and died. She had been trained as a nurse once upon a time and had gotten him drunk, then using a small needle, injected him with air into his blood stream. Once the air got to his heart, he died with convulsions. She was sure this would not be detected, which it wasn't, and she had gotten away with that one. Now she was sure she would get away with this. This time, though, it appeared that there were some questions about the death. The deputy had seen to it that the official report cleared her, but others didn't accept that. She had heard enough about Marty's brothers and friends that it bothered her. They could each one be very unpredictable and selflessly stand up for one another. She feared what one or more of them might do if they truly suspected her.

Rose had already decided that she had to leave the area and had been looking for a place. On the third day after shooting Marty, she loaded everything up and moved out. Her children had come back home the day before and helped her load everything. She left without telling the deputy she was going or where she was going. She had found an apartment on the other side of the state. The day before, she had overheard in the store some people talking, saying that Tony Carlton had sent word that he was going to hunt her down. He had also sent word that she had better not ever go to Texas. They also said that he was a Texas Ranger now, beads of sweat appeared on her forehead. For the first time in her life, she was afraid of the consequences of her actions. She got back in her car to go home, but her hands were sweating so that she could barely grip the steering wheel. The snare she had trapped Marty in seemed to be closing in around her.

Hastily Rose left the area, and for what anyone in that community ever knew, she disappeared, or at least for a long time. Troy, the deputy, didn't hear from Rose for days. He was being left out of all briefings about Marty. Each time he walked through the sheriff's office, the other deputies looked at him funny. He was afraid of what others might know. He went to Rose's house, but it was totally empty. She had moved with no forwarding information. He went to the post office and asked if she had left a forwarding address, to find out she hadn't, and they had several days mail piled up.

In the office, he overheard two other deputies talking about him, saying he might cause the whole department to come under state investigation. Troy thought that Rose had run out and left him holding the bag. Which she had done to him. He could feel a noose closing around his neck. He decided to pack up and move himself. He did so while his wife was away, taking everything he could load in his pickup and camper. He was never seen, or heard from again. He had decided to leave the state, going to a place he had heard of in west Texas. As Troy pulled out, leaving the county, another deputy called a Texas Ranger that he knew.

Nearly two weeks after his death, the autopsy report was finished. Marty's mother had to go and get a copy with a court order. She sat down to read the report and cried all the way through. It explained the route each bullet went through his body. The determination was that it took over forty minutes for him to bleed out and die. That death was due to massive blood loss. If he had received medical attention within the first thirty minutes, there was some probability that he could have survived. She had already asked for and received a written police report of the death. It stated that Rose had shot him in justifiable homicide. The time of her call about the shooting was only five minutes before his time of death, though. To her, this sounded like he had laid there bleeding for at least thirty-five minutes before she called. Why? Why wouldn't she have called right after the shooting if she was trying to protect herself? It just didn't make sense. Why had the deputy stopped him that close to home and only after four or five beers? Marty could drink much more and still drive straight. Now Rose had disappeared, as had the deputy. This all sounded to suspicious to her, but nobody would listen to her. The sheriff's department had already been having problems and didn't want to draw any more negative attention. This county had been listed as the easiest place to commit murder and get away with it. It was a black list that was humiliating the sheriff's department. They didn't want any more news reporters around, which an unsolved murder would bring in droves.

Another victory over the plans by Rose, Marty was buried in the family plot and not cremated. By the time the body was released from the autopsy, his mother had a court order for the body to be released to a funeral home of her choosing. His mother had help from Marty's friends, coworkers and family to see he had a proper burial. All of his family, brothers, and friends were there. Even Tony, who had come in from Texas. He was driving a Dodge truck with state of Texas plates. He wore a black hat, black jeans and a white shirt, with a black vest. Though not visible, some could tell that he carried a pistol and a badge under the vest.

After the funeral, Tony asked around if anyone knew where Rose had gone and why she wasn't there. Again, he spread the word for anyone that heard from her to inform her not to ever go into Texas. Before the day was over, that word had made its way to Rose. As the voice on the telephone relayed his words she trembled in fear. Though she had only met him once or twice, she had been told how unrelenting Tony could be. She vowed to herself that it would take an act of God to drop her into Texas, as she would never voluntarily go there.

Rose settled in but was always looking over her shoulder. Her son soon left to be on his own and never looked back. He didn't leave a number or tell his mom where he was going. Without warning, her other children soon left the same way. Between what conscious she had and the occasional word, that she was being hunted, her nerves were wearing thin on her.

One weekend before Christmas, a guy from the electric company was shopping with his family, at the mall in the city. He was sure he saw Rose and started toward her. The woman he saw looked a lot older now and ran away, disappearing in the crowd. Rose had gone to the mall and was surprised by seeing one of Marty's old friends. She turned and ran away as he had moved toward her. She was sure he would tell everyone that he had seen her and where at. Rose had a new job there and was on her way to work.

She would have to hide again. More and more, she was becoming paranoid. She moved to another town a few days later. This time, though, it was to a small town near the Texas border, but in Oklahoma.

The county sheriff was voted out of office the next election. Billy went with his mom, asking questions at the sheriff's office. No one would say a thing about the solved case, as they called it. His mother had sent letters to the lab that did the autopsy without any answer. She got a note from the attorney general's office once stating that the county had the authority over the case and they had closed it as a solved case. The results of the autopsy had been supplied to the investigating officer and the district attorney. Any further action was up to the county and or the district.

Billy and his mom had more questions. Some friends had told them that the deputy had been seen with Rose at a restaurant several times. This had been weeks before Marty had been arrested. What were they doing together? Why had that same deputy been the first one to the house after the shooting? Why had he disappeared shortly after she had? Were they together? What was this deputy's involvement with Rose and Marty's death?

*****

Many years later Billy, Larry, Tim and Tony were together for Kevin's funeral. They were talking together before the funeral and had asked Tony if he was still a Texas Ranger. He told them that he had retired a few years earlier. They asked him if he ever found out what happened to Rose. He smiled and all he would say was, "No one will ever know what happened to her."

The End

If you enjoy this story buy some of my other books. All available on Amazon and Kindle eBooks

Murder at Medicine Creek
A Tough Row to Hoe
Bitsy's First Deer Season
To Run With the Big Dogs
Legend of Indian Head Rock
Skyfish
The Day the Earth Stopped
Love Across the Creek
Society of Mars Exploration I
Society of Mars Exploration II
Society of Mars Exploration III
Society of Mars Exploration IV
Society of Mars Exploration   the complete series Hardback
Kaah Taak'in
Voyage to One Helluva Day

Watch for upcoming titles
Love Under the Lamp
Legend of Royals
The Empress and the Cyborg
Love to Murder

Made in the USA
Monee, IL
08 October 2024

66886928R00095